OASIS ONE
DANIEL WEISBECK

Publisher, Copyright, and Additional Information

Oasis One by Daniel Weisbeck, published by DJW Books

www.danielweisbeckbooks.com

Cover design by Rafael Andres

Edited by Lauren Humphries-Brooks

In loving memory of my mother, Margret Mary Hinkley.

For the reader, thank you for buying this book. Without you Doctor Mercy Perching would just be a name on a notebook.

CHAPTER ONE

In a windowless bedroom built for one, three people—or more specifically, two humans and one avian-human hybrid—were crowded together waiting for new life to take place. Doctor Mercy Perching, not a day over six months pregnant, lay huffing and puffing in her bed, anxious to bring her daughter into the world, even though she worried it would be a difficult life in the Sanctuary of Europe for the only human-canine.

"Breathe!" Basil urged Mercy, standing by her side, trying to sound confident.

"What do you think I am doing?" Mercy snapped back.

"Too much shout?" Basil said apologetically, his head cocked slightly to the left.

"Oh lord," Mercy moaned, panting hard and rolling her eyes. "Jillet, can you sing me through this please?"

The half-bird girl, wings for arms and a stubby yellow beak for a nose, stood next to Mercy on the right side of the bed. On cue, she began to whistle a soft, rhythmic tune. Breathing in and out in tempo with the melody, Mercy walked herself through to the end of her contraction. Relieved, exhausted, and already waiting for the next round of clenching pain, she collapsed against the wall at the top of her bed. Her knees raised and legs wide open, she was prepared to give birth any minute.

Agent Basil, a trained diplomat, seasoned in military manoeuvres, was suddenly rendered a helpless man in the face of childbearing.

"I am not sure about this anymore." Basil tossed the words out in a near panic. "You should be in the medical ward having a caesarean like all the other surrogates."

"You know why I'm not. If the Five Leaders find out my child is a hybrid, I won't even have ten minutes with her," Mercy answered, reminding him of the importance of their secret. "Gia, can you please give me a little more notice before the next contraction starts?" Mercy ordered her personal virtual assistant.

"Are you certain? Ten minutes ago, you asked me to not warn you in advance," the assistant's voice answered from the ether of the room.

"Alright, alright. Just tell me the stats then."

"Your foetus's heart rate is elevated, but still within an acceptable range. All other readings are normal. However— you sound agitated."

Basil and Mercy shot each other a look, and their lips spontaneously curled up into a burst of laughter. Their friendship had deepened over the six months of her pregnancy. At first, this newfound arrangement was out of necessity. Mercy needed someone she could trust. Someone close to the Five Leaders of the Sanctuary of Europe who could help her hide her unusual pregnancy.

"Oh…" Mercy screamed as her belly squeezed.

"Another contraction?" Basil asked nervously.

Mercy nodded her head fiercely, unable to speak. Her

perspiration-soaked hair lay pressed against her plump cheeks and her eyes squeezed shut.

"Breathe, just breathe," Basil coached, much more gently this time around.

"Ahhh!" Mercy screeched in pain. Something was not right.

"The foetus's heart rate is dropping," alerted Gia. "Agent Basil, we must call the doctor now."

"No!" Mercy cried as her white bedsheets turned red.

"Make the call, Gia," Basil ordered and started placing towels between Mercy's legs. "You're going to be okay, Mercy."

These were the last words she heard before the world around her went black.

CHAPTER TWO

MERCY WOKE. White, that was the first thing she saw—white ceilings and walls all around her. Clicks and beeps of machines came at her slowly, fading in and getting louder. Something pricked at her belly. As she tried moving her legs, a violent stabbing pain ripped through her torso. The throbbing released a flood of memories: images of her bed filling with blood, and Basil's face gone white. Her heart raced as adrenaline coursed through her veins.

"Where is she? Where is my baby?" Mercy stammered, forcing the words out of her dry mouth.

People standing around her came into focus. Two nurses on each side of her bed held her arms down as a doctor started flashing a light into her wide and terrified eyes. She brushed him away.

"Where is Basil?" she demanded.

Her eyes found him standing at the end of her bed. His face told her immediately her baby was gone.

"No! I want to see her. I need to see her!" Her plea grew more and more frantic.

"Give her another dose of the sedative," the doctor instructed the nurse on the right.

Swinging her arms outward, Mercy found her strength, and pushed at both nurses, causing them to stumble backward. The doctor put his hands on her shoulders. This was a mistake. With a single blow to his chest, he was also tripping back and into one of the nurses, sending her to the ground. Mercy locked eyes with Basil.

"I want to see her," she said in a steely voice. "I have to see her, Basil."

Basil hastened to her side. The doctor and nurses kept back.

"I'm so sorry," he said. "She…she didn't make it."

"Where is she? Did they take her to the lab? They will dissect her, tear her apart!"

Her mounting rage suddenly exploded into grief, and her sobs poured out like a tap turned on.

"I've asked them to keep the baby here until you woke," Basil told her calmly.

Mercy's hands covered her face, and she fell back into the bed. Her chest heaved as she tried desperately to control her crying. Slowly, breath by breath, she quieted and calmed her body. A numbed pain pulsated from her lower abdomen. The cut was already sealed shut and healed with a biogenerator. But the scar of her child lost would be with her forever.

After a few moments, her breathing steadied enough to talk again. She reached for Basil's hand. "Thank you. Thank you," she whispered. "I want to see her now, please."

Basil turned and spoke quietly to the doctor. Both nurses left the hospital room together. The doctor approached Mercy, this time standing an arm's length away should her fist explode again.

"The foetus's heart stopped before you delivered. There

was nothing anyone could do. Not even you," he said with well-rehearsed compassion.

"Do you know the cause?" Mercy asked.

"Not yet. We don't even understand the biology right now," he confessed.

Mercy nodded and turned her head away. There was nothing more to say.

The doctor took his leave after telling Mercy she could check out in the morning. Basil pulled up a chair and sat near her bed. They waited in silence. After a few minutes, one of the nurses returned, holding a tiny bundle close to her chest, swaddled in a blanket, the contents hidden from view. She gently handed the infant to Mercy, who received it as if it were the thinnest piece of glass that could break at any moment. Her hands trembled, and her throat closed in. She lifted the blanket and uncovered her naked child, curled in a ball, eyes closed. The baby's ears were long and pointed, like Chase, her human-canine father, and she had a patch of fine fur, still wet from being cleaned, clinging to her head and running all the way down her back. The tail just at the end of her spine came as no surprise to Mercy, who had seen the image of the tiny appendage wriggling in her natal scans. Her dark-skinned, porous nose, flat and puppy-like, was more human than Chase's.

Mercy reached down and held the tiny fingers, tipped with soft translucent claws. Leaning in closer, her lips caressed the cold cheeks of her stillborn daughter. The baby smelt fresh, like something new.

She couldn't help but wonder what classification her child would have been given back in the Sanctuary of Americas. Maybe a Classification 10 hybrid, like her father, the most animal features allowed in the human-animal mix. Any foetus ranked higher than C10 was terminated before birth. Her tail would have been problematic. A feature not allowed. But it was small, and Chase would have found a way to hide it from the world, protect his child.

Nearly twenty minutes passed when the nurse returned. Mercy looked the stranger in the eyes. "She is mine to examine. No other doctor or scientist is to touch her. Do you understand? No experiments." Her tone was fierce.

The nurse simply nodded and held out her arms. Mercy took one last look, pulled the blanket over her child's body and gifted her back to the nurse as gently as the baby had been received.

Basil stood. "Do you want to be alone?"

Mercy nodded and turned away, facing the empty wall.

"If there is anything you need, let me know. I'll come by tomorrow to pick you up."

Basil started following the nurse out of the room when Mercy turned back. "Wait. Close the door and come here please."

Basil did as she requested. They were alone.

"Are you in trouble with the Leaders?" she asked.

"No. They knew about your pregnancy and Chase. The Prime informed them a while back."

Surprised, Mercy sat forward. She should have expected as much. The Prime, the leader of the Sanctuary of Americas, had wanted her to terminate the pregnancy in an effort to hide the hybrids from the world. When Mercy escaped the Sanctuary pregnant, and with Jillet, the Prime came after them.

"And the Leaders aren't upset with you for hiding the truth?" she asked.

"I think you underestimate them. They are more concerned for your health than the politics of the situation," he said softly.

Mercy placed a hand on her empty belly and lay back, casting her eyes to the ceiling. Basil stood by her side quietly. The humming of medical equipment filled the profound silence between them. Its hypnotic noise allowed her to focus and collect her thoughts. All at once a determination stiffened her expression. She turned and locked eyes with Basil.

"Do me one last favour."

"Anything."

"Burn her."

Basil's face washed pale.

"You know they will not stop until they have pulled her apart and examined every last cell in her body. I don't care how you do it, just cremate her before they get to her. And bring me the ashes."

Basil nodded; the only answer possible. Mercy turned over in her bed, facing the wall, as he left the room.

* * *

The next morning Mercy checked out of the medical ward before Basil arrived. She could no longer bare the smells and sounds of her hospital room. Everything around her had come to represent death. She needed an early escape.

As she made her way to the nearest underground hyper-loop station, her thoughts turned to Jillet. Even though the child was only thirteen years old, her capacity to handle others' emotions empathetically was well beyond her years. Mercy had relied on the avian's unique singing gift for comfort more than once.

The first time Jillet had helped her, they were crawling through a barely human-size dirt tunnel under the mountain ranges of the Green Belt, a natural reserve in the Sanctuary of Americas. Deep in the belly of the Earth, she began to feel claustrophobic, terrified she would be buried alive. Jillet, just ahead of her, began to whistle a melody with a perfect syncopated rhythm, like a metronome. Mercy followed the notes, breathing in and out, crawling in step, until her panic dissipated.

This morning, Mercy had a similar suffocating feeling. Like the world was slipping out from under her feet while the ceiling collapsed over her. A song from Jillet might help.

Arriving at her apartment, Mercy found it empty. Basil must have already taken Jillet to the Department of Population Reclamation, where Mercy was head virologist. The avian child was the only known creature on the planet with a genetic immunity to the deadly FossilFlu virus mutation spreading across the Americas. Unlocking her DNA was a top priority for the Sanctuary of Europe, and the reason the Prime was willing to go to war to get her back.

Mercy stood at the foot of her doorway for a long moment with her memories of the last six months and the trauma of her recent loss, trying to make sense of it. Part of her was missing. She had an urge to run back, find her child and bring her home. The thought of stepping into her apartment without her baby gripped her heart and threatened to squeeze it dry.

How naive she was to believe she could prepare for this moment. The Prime had warned her that Classification 10 hybrid pregnancies rarely made it to term. A smart person, a logical person, a doctor even, should have been better prepared for this outcome.

Looking around the apartment, she noticed Basil had removed his personal items. Not that there were many. His moving in was a temporary measure to hide the truth about her pregnancy from the Five Leaders.

Something unusual caught the corner of her eye. A simple but elegant, polished silver box, no bigger than the width of two palms, sat at the centre of her dining table. She instantly knew what it was without opening it. Basil must have been able to convince the Leaders to allow the cremation. A surge of relief welled up in her body, followed by a tightening of her throat to hold back tears. Next to the box was a small handwritten note. She opened it and read aloud:

Dear Mercy,

As you requested. She is yours alone.

Your dear friend,

Bas

Mercy sat down at the table with the box laid in front of her. Her lower lip began to tremble as tears rose to her eyes and rolled over her cheeks. She already knew her next steps. She had decided in the hospital the moment she asked Basil to cremate her baby where she would bury the ashes. But when?

With shoulders curled forward, eyes unflinching, Mercy stared at the box, paralysed by indecision. After an hour of stillness, she began to move. Carefully picking up the metal case, she was surprised by its weight. It was much lighter than holding her baby back in the hospital. She walked it across her apartment and stood before a stunted orange tree. Years of keeping the orange tree alive had become a sort of ritual for Mercy. Proof that life can thrive, even in the most desperate of circumstances.

She placed the tiny coffin on a shelf above the tree and took several steps backward. Tilting her head to the right, she squinted and stepped forward again, twisting the container ever so slightly to the left. Satisfied, she stood for a few moments longer and then turned, making her way back to her bedroom.

Mercy undressed and stepped into her shower cubical. "Gia, on please. And don't turn the water off until I say so."

"Are you asking me to go beyond your daily ration of water for domestic use?"

"Exactly."

"The Department of Resource Allocation will be notified."

"Do it anyways."

"Understood."

A thin stream of water began to fall from the ceiling. She put her hands against the shower wall and leaned forward, letting the tepid liquid wash over her head. Small trivets of silver raced down her cheeks, over her shoulders, and slipped down between her swollen breasts, still waiting to feed her child. The veins of water continued downward, rolling over the muscles of her abdomen, down further, until touching the puffy red line just below her belly button, sending an explosive shudder across her skin. She ran a finger over the tender flesh. Pushed at it, causing a sharp jolt of pain. She poked it again, harder this time, wanting to feel the soreness, wanting to never forget it was there.

Showered, dressed, and waiting for Jillet to come home, she sat in her living room growing increasingly uncomfortable with the suffocating despair pressing down on her. Unsure what to do next, she defaulted to the one constant in her life: her work.

"Gia, run through unopened comms."

The assistant's voice recited: "You have ten unheard but not urgent messages from your lab relating to tests on Jillet and your notes on FossilFlu mutation. A condolence message from the Council of Leaders. A note from Basil to call when ready. And a message from Tommy."

Mercy's eyes shot open as she bolted forward, causing a sharp ache in her stomach. "Ouch!" she yelped, clinging to her belly and quickly sitting back down. "Gia, why didn't you tell me there was a message from Tommy?" she snapped.

Tommy was the code name for Joan, her friend and the leader of the rebels against the Prime, used to send secret messages to Mercy. These were one-way messages, as Mercy had no way of contacting Joan. The hybrid rebels were constantly on the move, hiding in the mountains of the Sanctuary's Green Belt.

This was the third message from Joan in six months. The first arrived just weeks after Mercy returned to the Sanctuary of Europe. It was a warning. Joan had intelligence the Prime was sending a battalion of hybrid soldiers to fight for Jillet's return, should the Five Leaders refuse to give her up. The early information allowed the Sanctuary of Europe enough time to prepare a defence. The Prime was caught off guard when the Sanctuary's war ships met her advance out at sea, forcing both sides into a stalemate.

The second message was another warning and a request. The deadly FossilFlu virus was spreading rapidly across the Sanctuary's reserves. Animals all across the Green Belt were dying. The Sanctuary city was in lockdown, shutting the rebels out and leaving them exposed. A vaccine was needed quickly.

Mercy's stomach turned at the thought of what might be in this new message. "Gia, decrypt and read the communication."

"Message received at fourteen hundred hours yesterday. It reads: *Things regarding the virus have worsened. The Prime is allowing the virus to spread in the Belt as a way of eradicating the rebels. Death is everywhere. Only a few rebels are still alive and uninfected. I have no choice but get the last of us out. The Prime's military is all around your city, so we are going to the Sanctuary of Asia until things calm down...Mercy, should this be our final communication, I must confess something. I don't know how to tell you this other than to just say it. Chase did not die in the battle on the mountain. He is with us and still alive. He constantly worries about your safety and refuses to let me tell you. But this is a different world we are living in now, and I thought you should know. Take care, my friend.*

May we be lucky enough to see each other again someday. End of message."

Mercy's throat went dry. "He's alive?" she repeated under her breath. *But how?* Her face flushed red as she rapidly tapped the heal of her foot on the floor. *Why didn't he contact me? Come for me?* Her heart beat louder and faster. Anger, joy, sadness, hope—they all rushed at her so fast she had to stand. Her hands were trembling. She gave them a shake, trying to calm herself. She needed to think.

Pacing the room, she recalled the horrific details of the last time she had seen Chase, kneeling on the edge of the mountain cave, a laser bullet shot to his chest. Athena had flown down from the sky above and swooped her up, pulled her away from him. She did not want to go. She wanted to die with him. Now he was alive and in trouble. Mercy suddenly knew what she had to do.

"Gia, call Basil."

A miniature image of an anxious Basil appeared over the holographic generator in her desk.

"I'm glad you called," he rushed out, not waiting for her to greet him. "Are you okay? You were gone when I arrived. I thought we had agreed to—"

"Bas," she interrupted. "Stop, it's okay. I'm fine."

"Really?"

"Listen, I need you to come over. I've received another message from Joan."

"I'm on my way." His image evaporated.

After a long twenty-minute wait, Basil finally arrived, letting himself in and rushing to her side.

Mercy was sitting on her sofa, twisting her hands white. She attempted to stand.

"Don't get up," he ordered as he joined her on the lounge.

"Basil, the news isn't good," she burst out. "The virus is

spreading and it's no longer safe for the rebels to stay at the Sanctuary of Americas."

"Do they want to come here?"

"No. Joan is worried about escalating the situation with the Prime. She's taking the last of the fugitives to the Sanctuary of Asia."

Basil sat back, surprised. "The Sanctuary of Asia has refused contact with the outside world for the last one hundred years. How did Joan get through to them?"

"I don't know. But–" Mercy grabbed Basil's hands and held him in place. "Bas, I want to bring them here. I need to go to the Sanctuary of Asia."

Basil jumped to his feet, as she expected. "What! No, Mercy, not now, not after…well not ever, really. It's way too dangerous. I need to tell the Leaders about the message. We have to. Let the Sanctuary send ships out to find Joan."

"You know we can't do that. If you tell the Leaders, there is a chance it will get back to the Prime through her spies. It will put their lives in danger. We have to do this on our own."

"Us!"

"You're right, Bas, I can't go…not alone. But you can come with me. We can find Joan and bring her and the rest of the fugitives back here."

Basil began a hard pace back and forth, rubbing his hand across his forehead as Mercy's eyes followed him relentlessly. She took hope from the fact that he had not rejected her request outright. Several painful moments passed before he stopped walking and spoke again.

"There is no point arguing with you, is there?"

Mercy pursed her lips and gave her head a stubborn shake.

"I need time to think. Promise me you will wait. You will not do anything rash."

Mercy reluctantly agreed but insisted on an answer by the

end of the day. As Basil left, she felt a pang of guilt not telling him Chase was alive. She sensed for some time that Basil's feelings for her were deepening beyond friendship. Telling him about Chase would only complicate things. No, she convinced herself, better to share the truth about Chase later, after he agreed to help her.

CHAPTER THREE

MERCY SPENT the day preparing for the trip she knew Basil could not refuse her.

By late afternoon, she was sitting at her desk in absorbed concentration, preparing notes to leave with her lab, when a soft breathy whistle came at her from behind. Turning, she found Jillet staring at her anxiously.

"Hello you." Mercy smiled.

Jillet tweeted and pointed the tip of her right wing at Mercy's belly.

Mercy's throat tightened as she fought back a cry. "I'm okay. There is nothing for you to worry about."

A single tear fell down Jillet's cheek and rolled off her little yellow beak of a nose. Mercy pulled her into a long, comforting hug. She knew the loss was as real for Jillet as it was for her. Having another hybrid in the Sanctuary would have given the bird-girl some respite from her isolation. Now that the baby was gone, she was destined to a life among only humans. Mercy realized she had no choice but to tell Jillet about the possibility of reuniting with Joan and the other hybrids.

"Have a seat." Mercy indicated toward the sofa and joined her. "I've received some news from Joan."

Jillet's eyes widened as she let out a quick, low chirp, something Mercy had come to know as concern.

"It's not good news." Mercy hesitated. "The virus is spreading in the Belt. But Joan and Athena are okay, for now. They have decided to leave the Sanctuary."

Jillet perked up, blowing a series of whistles ending on high notes.

Mercy guessed her meaning. "No, they are not coming here. Joan is worried about putting us in danger."

Jillet's enthusiasm quickly dampened into a near pout.

"However," Mercy took a long breath. "I'm going to find them and bring them back to live with us. Basil will be joining me…I hope. But we have to go right away. Do you understand?"

Jillet nodded in fierce agreement and pointed her wingtip to her chest.

"No." Mercy shook her head. "It's too dangerous. I can't take you."

The avian child bolted up from the sofa and slammed her claw foot to the ground, letting out several high, piercing shrieks.

"You won't change my mind. I'm not letting you go. And don't get any ideas about sneaking along. I know how clever you can be."

The girl crossed her wings in front of her and turned her face away in anger.

Mercy reached for her. "I know you want to help. But I need you to stay here. I can't bear the thought of losing another child."

They both stopped short at her confession. It was the first

time Mercy had openly referred to Jillet as her child. Jillet met Mercy face to face, examining her for the truth. Mercy sat in eager silence. With a flap of her wings, Jillet swaddled Mercy into a cocoon of feathers.

"That's right, we are family now. And I won't let anything happen to you," Mercy whispered in her ear.

"Did I miss something," came a voice, startling them.

There Basil stood, holding a small travel bag and a crooked smile.

Mercy beamed with delight. "Are you sure?"

Basil nodded his head confidently. Jillet ran to his side and embraced him.

"I've told Jillet everything," Mercy said. "Now, we just need to figure out what to tell my lab."

"I've already taken care of that," he said, making it clear this was now his operation. "I've explained you need some time to yourself and not to contact you for a few days. Considering the circumstances, they understood without question. I've also booked a ship to attend my quarterly tour of the farming reclamation project outside the city. It's a month early, but nobody will think twice about it. The cover should work as long as we get back within a few days. Any longer and it will look suspicious."

Mercy held back an urge to run and join their hug. "Thank you, Bas. I really don't know how I could have gotten through any of this without you."

"You should go rest. We leave early tomorrow morning."

As she walked down the hall, she heard Basil ask Jillet about her day. They had an odd way of understanding each other, even if they did not share a language. It was sweet. How lucky they were to have Basil.

Back in her room, Mercy lay on her bed and stared at the ceiling. Her mind spun with thoughts of Chase. Memories of their first night together rushed through her body: the touch of his hands, his warm lips, the sloppy puppy dog eyes he gave her when he thought she would reject him for being a hybrid. She imagined he was lying next to her. She tried to tell him about their baby, but there were no words to explain it, not yet. Reaching down, she caressed the scar beneath her gown. She longed to bury herself in the cavity of his arms and lose herself against his chest. How different the last few days could have been if he were here. Not easier, but perhaps less lonely.

Mercy's bones grew heavy and sunk deeper into the soft cushion of her bed. Her mind began to sway on the edge of sleep, dipping in and out. Slowly, she welcomed the calm void where her worries were far away.

The next morning, Mercy woke in the middle of a dream. She was standing outside a house looking in through a window. Chase and their baby were inside playing. The child was older, maybe eight or nine. There was laughter and a little growling as he teased her—human and dog noises in equal measure. Something dark and sinister lurked behind her. The entity, without shape, only gravity, started pulling her away from them. Mercy was shouting, pounding on the glass to get Chase's attention when she woke herself.

The dark force separating her from Chase and their daughter followed her into the waking world. For a fraction of a moment, she lay confused. So vivid was the dream, and so real was the child, that she wondered if the horrific events of the last few days were in fact the nightmare and her daughter was alive. Mercy placed a hand on her flat belly. The stab of pain in her lower abdomen left no doubt about which world was real. *But Chase, Chase is alive. That wasn't a dream. And he needs my help.* She jumped out of bed and quickly changed into her clothes.

Basil and Jillet were waiting for her in the living room. It was late morning, and Jillet should have already been off to the lab.

"Why didn't you wake me?" Mercy directed her frustration at Basil. She turned to Jillet. "Does the lab know you're coming in late?"

Basil answered for her. "Yes, I've told them to expect her shortly."

Mercy squatted on her haunches, meeting Jillet face to face. Tucking a few loose strands of the girl's auburn hair behind her ear, she spoke sternly but gently. "Please promise me you will listen to Peter in the lab. Gia will be with you all the time and can get you anything you need." Mercy looked up at Basil. "Maybe she should just stay with Peter?"

Jillet placed her hands on Mercy's shoulder and blew a confident whistle into the air. Mercy knew she was right. After all, Jillet had escaped from a military camp and hid in the wild jungles of the Green Belt for months on her own. She could handle a few days alone in the safety of the Sanctuary.

"Mercy, we have to get going," Basil reminded her.

She gave Jillet a long, firm hug. "Okay, off with you. I promise we will be back shortly with Joan and—" She caught herself mid-sentence before saying Chase, and quickly corrected the near gaff. "…With the rest of the fugitives." Luckily, neither of them seemed to notice.

Jillet grabbed one last look back before exiting the apartment, leaving Mercy with a feeling of abandoning the child. The wave of guilt only fuelled her determination. *I promise, I will be back.*

* * *

Basil led the way to the transport hub. They travelled on foot through a series of back alleys and hidden hallways Mercy had no idea even existed. The clandestine nature of their movement, more a slinking than a walk, made her briefly question his confidence in the plan.

"Ouff!" Mercy bleated as she bumped into Basil, who had come to a sudden stop. "What is it?"

"We are being followed," he said in a barely audible voice.

Mercy listened intently. Then she heard it. The sound of feet lightly shuffling in the hallway behind them. The noise disappeared. Whoever was following them must have stopped. Basil looked her in the eyes and shook his head to say, *don't move and stay quiet.* In a flash he was gone, his suitcase sitting at her feet.

Several minutes passed in agonising stillness. Mercy began to wonder what was the worst that could happen if someone stopped them. They had not actually left the Sanctuary, which of course was forbidden without Council approval. A prison sentence waited for anyone caught outside the city walls without permission.

The quiet broke with the sound of someone running in her direction. Mercy's heart leapt into her throat. Her gaze dashed in every direction, looking for a place to hide. She was helplessly exposed. Basil appeared from around the corner to her relief.

"Who was it?" she asked.

"I didn't see anyone. They must have heard me coming and doubled back." He sounded more annoyed than scared.

"Do you think it could be Jillet?"

"No, I contacted Peter to check. She is in the lab."

"Do you think it's one of the Prime's spies?"

"Likely. I've had suspicions I'm being followed ever since you came back."

"What! You're only telling me this now? Is that why we are sneaking around?"

"Later." He brushed her questions aside. Reaching down and opening his case, he pulled out a green bodysuit with a gold foil helmet, the uniform of a reclamation farm worker. "Put this on. We are getting close to the station."

Farm work and mining were some of the least desirable jobs in the Sanctuary of Europe. Travelling in and out of the city increased exposure to solar radiation. Hence the full-body uniforms and helmets. Even with advanced medical treatments, many farmers eventually ended up with hair loss, radiation sickness, or even cancer. But the credits earned for farming were some of the highest in the city. It was a gambler's job, and as such, attracted a particular type of person. The kind of person soldiers working in the ship bays would not pay much attention to as long as they had the right paperwork. Basil had found the perfect disguise. Mercy quickly changed and they continued down the hall.

The transport hub was noisy with the usual daily activities of the Sanctuary's mining and farming industries. Bleating sirens announced a constant flow of incoming and outgoing hovercrafts and landships. Clanking metal confirmed ships locked into holding bays, ready to be unloaded. Whirring conveyor belts carried ceaseless processions of cargo containers along the length of the vast hall, until dropping them into hyperloop tunnels to be dispensed throughout the underground city. Glass eye drones zipped through the air, diligently scanning and cataloguing the containers and ships, ensuring nothing was stolen, hidden or damaged.

Basil entered the transport hub first, with Mercy following close behind. She kept her head down and face in the shadows of her helmet. At the bay's entrance was a large round control centre manned by several government workers dressed in all white bodysuits and red helmets. A tall holographic screen beamed up from the countertop separating the transport officials from visitors. This was the first checkpoint where travel permissions were validated. Behind the control centre was a security gateway heavily guarded by soldiers. The long bank of waist-high pylons emitting holographic barriers were busy flashing green, confirming travel permission for those on the go, and clearing those on return as FossilFlu free. Large crowds mingled on both sides of the gateway, alighting with the casualness of daily routines. The constant murmur and calm nature of their conversations helped Mercy compose herself.

"Agent Basil, nice to see you again," said one of the attendants behind the counter of the main control centre.

Basil nodded. "Is my ship ready?"

"Yes, you're in holding bay 230-1."

Basil offered the official his code for travel verification. The solider scrolled through the digital roster illuminated in front of him and input the data. One small box lit green.

"I'm sorry, Agent Basil. There is no indication of a second passenger on this log?"

Mercy's palms went damp and her breathing hastened. Her eyes darted left and right as she looked for an escape route should she need it.

"Wait," the solider interrupted himself. "There she is." He indicated the screen. "Strange. Ms Julie Constance, you are listed as cargo." His eyes tried to meet Mercy's directly.

"It was a late entry," Basil quickly interjected. "It must have been my assistant's error."

The transport agent's palpable silence drew a bead of sweat from Mercy's forehead. Finally, as if he never had any doubts, the agent smiled and said, "Certainly, no problem Agent Basil. I've made the change. You can proceed." The soldier waved them to the security check point.

Basil walked through the electronic passage to a green

light and waited on the other side. Mercy hesitated at first and then practically skipped through the digital panel. Green. She smiled in relief and stopped holding her breath.

"That was a close call," Mercy said once they were well past security and comfortably indistinguishable from the hundreds of other workers filing through the bay.

"I had to slip you in as cargo to avoid pre-boarding verification checks. I knew they wouldn't question us at the counter. Not a direct agent of the Third Leader." He smiled.

Safely aboard their hovercraft, the government agent and the farmworker shared a cautious smile.

"Strap yourself in," Basil ordered, and waved a hand over the ship's helm, illuminating a large digital control panel.

The golden ship levitated upward and glided past the shaded threshold of the docking bay, and into the unknown.

CHAPTER FOUR

THE GREAT FORTY-FOOT wall surrounding the Sanctuary of Europe slipped under the horizon as Basil and Mercy's ship continued to sail eastward.

Above them, the sky was a barren expanse of blue. Below, cargo ships on land and in the air created a river of traffic along the otherwise repetitive and desolate desert landscape. With the Prime's army sitting at the ready in the westward sea, the Sanctuary had significantly increased military presence along the mining routes. Basil and Mercy flew in a held silence, not willing to relax until safely past the last point of civilisation.

After nearly an hour in the air, Mercy jutted forward and squinted. She spotted something rising out of the golden dunes and waves of heat. As they drew closer a ridge of white appeared on the skyline. They had finally reached the Sanctuary's Land Reclamation and Farming Project.

Basil twisted at the light dials on the floating control panel, slowing the hovercraft for their approach. The enormous project was now in full sight. Rows and rows of self-contained biodomes spread across the vista, some twenty miles wide and long, like giant beetles in marching order. Sitting adjacent to the greenhouses were a series of windowless monolithic stone buildings that served as permanent living quarters for government soldiers. The bleached barracks also provided safety for the farmers, who worked on strictly timed shifts of two hours on and off, to reduce exposure to radiation.

Mercy could not help but compare the bleak farming project with the Sanctuary of Americas' vast agricultural zones, miles of golden crops and evergreen orchards covering sways of healthy Earth, made possible by their Shade technology. A knot turned in her stomach at the thought of the Prime allowing all of it to be abandoned just to kill the rebels, while the citizens of the Sanctuary of Europe were risking their lives, scratching at the dry surface of the desert for meagre returns. The importance of finding Joan and Chase was made all the clearer. They knew the Shade. They could help her city prosper. If only she could find them.

A ringing from the ship's helm hailed Basil and Mercy. Basil entered his security codes, giving ground control access to the ship's AI for verification. Packets of encrypted data scrolled across the helm's screen. Basil opened an audio channel.

"Welcome, Agent Basil," came a female voice.

"Thank you."

"We've prepared your bay for docking."

Mercy shot Basil a concerned glare.

"We've had a change of plans," Basil started. "I'll be joining the eastern mining explorations first."

There was a momentary pause from the other side. "I'm sorry, but your passenger is only certified for the Land Reclamation facilities. Mining certificates require biometric DNA authentication."

"Yes, I'm aware. But I've just discovered that Ms Constance is quite the self-taught geologist," he said lightly. "I've agreed to let her travel along for educational purposes. She will be observing only. You can use my authorisation code to override permissions."

Another pause. Mercy was on the edge of her seat. Basil fanned his hand at her, a silent *it will be okay*. But his eyes were nervous.

"Certainly, Agent. That's all gone through," said the transport guard. "Please remember, hazsuits are mandatory from this point on if you disembark. You'll be outside of the scrub zone."

"Understood. Thank you, soldier." Basil closed the audio link. A grin of relief erupted across his face. "We're clear."

Mercy collapsed back into her seat. "Basil Goodman, I could hug you."

Basil's dark-skinned face burned a deep scarlet red, followed by an awkward moment of silence.

Mercy was quick to change the subject. "How long before we reach the Sanctuary of Asia?"

"We should arrive around dawn." He glanced at her from the corner of his eye. "You can take off the uniform now... unless you're thinking of a new career?" he teased.

Mercy rolled her eyes and unbuckled her harness. Slipping into the back of the cabin, she removed the heavy green farmer's uniform and changed into her own clothing. Watching Basil from behind, his thick black hair tucked neatly into a fish-tail braid, his soft brown skin and muscular build, she was reminded that once she had been attracted to him. Basil was assigned to be her government point of contact during her trip to the Sanctuary of Americas. They spent several days together debriefing for the mission. This was the supposed moment where she had become pregnant, or so they told the Leaders. But the reality was, there was no time for flirting back then. She had a deadly virus to stop, and he had two days to get a scientist, with no background in government diplomacy, ready to be the first person in one hundred years to visit the Sanctuary of Americas.

As Mercy pulled her beige bodysuit up over her shoulders a pang of guilt squeezed at her heart. This was the perfect moment to tell Basil about Chase. But something held her back. Something more than the mission. Revealing the truth would end the illusion of the last six months: a mother and father—and their daughter. The lie was the only memory of her child she had. She selfishly granted herself one more day to keep her family alive. Basil would understand.

Mercy pulled her sandy blond hair back into a simple knot and joined Basil at the helm.

"Basil…" She paused.

"Yes?"

"Back in the Sanctuary you said you had suspicions about the Prime's spy?"

Basil expression was sharp. "If I tell you, your life could be in danger. So, let's leave it for now."

Mercy almost laughed. "You don't think we are already in a little danger here? We have stolen a ship from the government. We are going to a city that we know next to nothing about. And we are travelling alone across one of the most dangerous landscapes on the planet."

The left corner of Basil's mouth slipped up. He shook his head. "This is insane, isn't it?"

"So? Who is it?"

"The First," he confessed on a long breath out, as if he were holding it in against his will.

Mercy's smile dropped, and all humour evaporated as her eyes grew wide with astonishment. "One of the Five Leaders is a spy?"

"Think about it. The kind of information the Prime was

able to gather on you and your lab work on the virus was highly classified. If there was any contact with the Sanctuary of Americas, it would have gone through the First."

The First Leader, in charge of the department of Information and Communication, was the youngest of the Five Leaders. A short, pudgy, bald figure, he had ice blue eyes and a permanent drip of sweat falling down his forehead. He carried with him a white cloth tucked in the sleeve of his red Leader's cloak, frequently pulling it out to dab the salty leak away—always unsuccessfully, for the next dribble was right behind it. If anyone was looking for a nervous spy, he fit the description.

"Now that you say it, yes, he does seem the most obvious. So why hasn't the Third questioned him?" The Third Leader was in charge of Security and Health.

"You don't question a Leader without evidence. He is very good at covering his tracks and has allies throughout the city."

"But why would one of the Leaders turn on his own people? What's there to gain?"

Then it hit her. The Prime's hybrid military: the size of the troops, the vast arsenal of weapons and machines. Her ambitions were always right in front of Mercy to see.

"He was helping the Prime plan a war." She spoke her thoughts out loud.

Basil nodded. "Yes, most likely. When you brought Jillet to our Sanctuary, things got complicated for her. We believe she had planned to let the virus spread and then use the promise of immunity to force us to surrender. The First was probably hoping to gain from her win."

"How will you stop him?"

"We need more evidence. We need a witness."

A pensive silence filled the ship. Mercy's brow knit tight in thought. Seconds turned into minutes, when, out of nowhere,

Mercy's eyes mushroomed, and she slapped her hands on the helm.

"You…" she hollered in an accusatory voice.

Basil turned, eyes wide, a little startled by her loudness. "What?"

"I'm so stupid," she said, shaking her head.

"What?" Basil insisted.

"That was way too easy. Getting permission to leave the Sanctuary so quickly and being allowed to take a ship with an undocumented worker on board." She wanted to laugh, but anger was bubbling to the surface. "Not even you could have pulled that off without questions. You told the Leaders about Joan. Joan is the witness they want!"

Basil's face burned red. He refused to look her in the eye. "I only told the Third. I promise."

"Why? Why lie to me, Bas?"

"I wanted to tell you. As soon as you shared the message from Joan with me, I wanted to tell you everything. But I have a job that requires my confidentiality. You always knew that." His tone begged for forgiveness.

"The Third and only the Third knows we are going to get Joan and the fugitives? There is no risk the First can find out and put Joan's life in danger?"

"Only the Third knows about Joan. I promise. And I trust her. She brought me into her confidence when we received the invitation to send you to the Sanctuary of Americas. We had hoped your trip would provide some evidence of the First's motives for turning against his own country."

"That's why you were assigned to watch over me?"

"Originally, yes."

For a long sickening second Mercy could not speak to him. "I thought you were my friend." Her face burned. "All this time, you've been spying on me. Everything has been one big lie?"

Basil sheepishly held her stare. "It wasn't *all* a lie."

Mercy violently turned forward, crossed her arms over her chest, and stared out into the bleak sandscape.

Several hours passed without conversation. Basil glanced over at her, more than once without return. When he realised Mercy was not going to talk to him, he finally spoke. "I can promise, it was the Prime and not me who informed the Leaders you were pregnant with a hybrid, if that is what you are wondering," he blurted out. "I would have never betrayed your secret." The topic was clearly weighing heavy on his mind.

Mercy cupped her forehead into the palm of her right hand and rubbed fiercely, as if battling a headache. She tried to ignore him. But something in his tone caught at her. Something she could not fight. Turning, she finally acknowledged his pleading gaze. What she saw was not a liar. She saw the man who stood by her bed while she was giving birth. The man in her kitchen, joking with Jillet. And the only person she trusted to deliver her daughter's ashes. Suddenly, she felt childish for behaving so badly, and her anger slipped away.

"I'm sorry as well," Mercy said. "I know you're trying to help me and do your job at the same time. It's just been a horrible few days. And I guess it's better to have the Third on our side than sending military ships out looking for a stolen hovercraft."

Basil nodded. "Indeed."

"Do you have any information on the Sanctuary of Asia at all?" Mercy was desperate to change the subject.

"Not much. They were the first Sanctuary to cut off communication after the FossilFlu pandemic. The Council has made several attempts to open dialogue over the years, but they've remained hostile to any attempts at contact."

Mercy shook her head disapprovingly. "I will never understand humans. There are so few of us left on this burned rock, and we still can't work together. The technology I've seen in the Americas could transform the planet for everyone. They had snow, Bas. Real snow. And freshwater rivers and lakes."

"What did it feel like? Being around rain and snow?" His voice was childlike.

"Like ice, but everywhere. Even your skin felt frozen. Ice crystals grew on your eyelashes, and your lungs grew cold with each breath." Mercy shivered just at the thought of it.

"Sounds nice," said Basil.

"You'll get to feel it one day, Bas. I know Chase and Joan will help us design a Shade of our own."

Basil sat back and cocked his head. "Chase is with Joan? I thought he was dead!"

It was Mercy's turn to flush red. Her confession spilled out hurriedly. "I'm sorry, Bas. I should have told you. I didn't know he was alive until yesterday. He refused to let Joan tell me. I guess he was worried I would risk my safety trying to find him."

"You mean like you are doing now," Basil quipped angrily.

Mercy's back straightened. "I guess we both have something to gain out of this trip," she snapped defensively.

Clearly bruised, Basil busied himself at the helm controls, ignoring Mercy. As they reached the end of the dry earth and the deep blue-green ocean filled the horizon, a second long silence separated them.

CHAPTER FIVE

OUTSIDE, the ocean sky was a starry black night. A thin arc of scarlet on the horizon teased the coming sunrise.

Inside, Basil continued to angrily punch away at the holographic helm. An unnecessary task, as the ship basically flew itself.

Mercy busied herself with work. Over the hours they had been at sea, she practiced several attempts at reconciliation with Basil in her head. But every time she tried to speak, the look of him got her angry and defensive again. She started to worry they might both be stubborn enough to never talk to each other again, when Basil suddenly broke his silence.

"That's strange," he said.

Mercy looked up and noticed that the ocean below had become rough. "Is there a storm coming?"

"This wasn't on any scans. There should have been a warning."

The sea below them began to violently churn, growing in strength with each sway backward and forward. Giant swells of water rose high out of the ocean and crashed down in white-capped fury. There was a loud *CRACK* like lightning from outside, immediately followed by a metallic *THUNG* as the ship violently veered to one side.

"What's that!" Mercy shouted, grabbing hold of the helm and trying not to fly out of her seat.

Basil urgently swiped at the flashing lights on the navigation screen, trying to gain control of the swinging ship. "We've been hit by some kind of charge. Strap yourself in," he ordered.

Mercy fumbled and pulled the safety belt around her waist and up over her shoulder. Directly in front of the ship, a blinding shaft of light shot up from the water and into an empty sky. And then another.

"That looks like lightning," Mercy exclaimed. "But it's coming from the ocean."

Flashing red lights and alarm bells bleated throughout the ship. Basil's face tightened as he desperately adjusted the holographic control panel. "Why didn't the ship detect this before?"

"What?" Mercy cried, holding on to her shoulder strap with white fingers.

"Something is under the surface of the water. I think this is some kind of man-made..." Before Basil could finish, another bolt clipped the rear of the ship, sending them both jarring forward into their belts with a hard snap when the hovercraft autocorrected. Mercy screamed in pain as her shoulder nearly dislocated.

"We're being attacked," Basil warned. "Ship, ascend! Now! Ascend!" But it was too late.

KABOOM! Mercy's head went fuzzy. A high-pitched ringing pierced her ears. Basil was screaming something at her, pointing to her seat, but she could not hear him. The wind whipped through the cabin, tearing her hair in every direction. As she turned around, she saw the source. A gaping hole at least a meter across had been burned straight through the floor of the ship. They were losing altitude, and the heaving sea was approaching too quickly to react.

The impact against the water was a hard crash rather than a sinking as Mercy expected. A loud, slow, metallic groan broke through the deafening winds as the ship was torn in half. Mercy and Basil were now in separate sections. Basil was limp, strapped into his seat, head loosely careening left, and right, and back again repeatedly. The blood drained from Mercy's face and her heart palpitated wildly. Water poured in, surrounding her feet. She screamed and screamed at Basil, but he was either injured or dead. Her fingers fumbled with the belt holding her prisoner to her seat, desperately trying to free herself as the water swallowed her legs. Images of Chase, her baby in her arms, and Jillet flashed before her eyes. The world felt as if it were simultaneously moving in slow motion yet rapidly running out of time. Basil's half of the ship was still above water, savagely tossed around by the larger than life waves. That was the last image Mercy saw of him before her head sunk below the water's surface.

In a frenzy, she continued to tear at the tight seatbelt. Her swollen lungs clung to her last breath, until, no longer able to hold the air in, she opened her mouth, releasing a flute of large bubbles. A reflexive gag forced her to draw in water, filling her lungs with sea. Her body, quickly realizing the mistake, automatically drew in once again, looking for oxygen. Her eyes swelled, and her chest spasmed twice before all of her body went limp. Her legs and arms pulled upward without resistance as the ship slipped further down into the abyss below.

With eyes still searching, and mind still conscious, her

breathing stopped. A calm surrender arrested her fear. In the fading light overhead, the image of a child appeared. It was her child, but older, running gleefully in a room, followed by a laughing Chase. Mercy smiled and closed her eyes, carrying the image of her family with her as she sunk deeper, into the forever night.

CHAPTER SIX

THE OUTLINE of a female human filled the ceiling to floor digital screen. Inside the figure, dense branches representing the voluminous human nervous and cardiovascular system were glowing neon green. Behind the body's wiring and tubes lay the organs in full 3D illustration. The heart, liver, and kidneys were also lit up in green light. Upward, into the skull, a model of a human brain was coloured in pulsating shades of orange to red.

Mercy's eyes slowly rolled open at the sound of a heartbeat coming from somewhere behind her. A sense of disconnection, of floating even, started to fade as the weight of her flesh and bones pulled her back to the ground. Her chest moved up and down in a steady pattern that felt familiar, like breathing. A tingling in her toes and fingertips crawled up her arms and legs until her entire body vibrated. Like a light switch flipping on, memories of being cold, the rancid taste of sea water in her mouth, and darkness rushed into her mind.

Mercy let out a loud, desperate gasp for air as her chest

jumped off the soft mattress underneath her. This time her lungs filled with oxygen. It was real. She was alive. Her eyes darted around as she tried to summon powers of logic from the murky, dream-like cloud blocking her mind. She was lying in a bed at the centre of a small room made up of four glass walls. Twisting her head back over her shoulder, she saw the ceiling to floor monitor charting her medical condition. The human brain, once red, now yellow, confirmed the subject was awake and improving.

She tried to sit up, only to be snapped back down against the mattress by straps tying her wrists to silver railings. Twisting her body, she discovered two more straps holding her ankles firmly in place. Pulling upward hard, she wrenched and contorted her wrists and feet, trying to free herself. Adrenaline sent her heart racing and sharpened her mind.

"Hello?" she cried. "Where am I?" Her voice sounded raspy; her throat was sore. The brightly lit room remained eerily silent. "Hello?" she screamed again. "Is anyone there?"

"Patient Alpha is conscious," came a male voice from behind the ceiling, giving Mercy a start. "Heart rate is elevated, and breathing is rapid. Subject is showing signs of distress and disorientation, but bodily organs, including cognitive functions, are stable. Fertility remains high. Harvesting may commence."

"What! Harvesting? I want to talk to whoever is in charge!" Mercy's hands tugged at the railings, and her head twisted around, trying to find any sign of a human. The room was empty. White opaque glass walls hid all views outside.

A tingling vibration raced through her bones as her body was suddenly pulled rigid against the bed. Madly, her eyes stared up at the ceiling, unable to move. Three large robot operating arms appeared from somewhere high and levitated over to her. The first, holding a thin needle the length of a fingernail, hummed as it twisted, bent, and leaned into her face. Four tiny pinchers surrounding the needle expanded and with precision tucked under her upper and lower right eyelids, stretching the skin away from her eyeball. Her dead lips tried to call out, scream. But all that came was a loud gurgling of vowels and hissing. *Pop!* The needle made a tiny barely audible noise as it broke through the rubbery surface of her eyeball.

The second drone arm, now hovering over her belly, squeezed out a needle five times the length of the first, and pierced her lower abdomen.

The third, positioned between her paralysed legs, pushed a small hose tip up into her uterus. Mercy's muffled screams grew louder and louder; white foam and spit spilled messily out of the corners of her mouth.

After a few moments, and an uncomfortable sucking feeling between her legs, the three surgical robot arms retracted, and slipped back up into the corners of the small chamber. Suddenly the bone-tickling humming ceased, and Mercy's muscles sprung loose. A wheezing noise sifted up from the floor, like the sound of pressurised air releasing, and a sickening metallic smell crept into her nose. Before she fell asleep, she imagined Jillet whistling something sweet.

CHAPTER SEVEN

BEEP—BEEP—BEEP. The sounds of monitors, and heart-beats, and breathing—her breathing, woke Mercy. Turning her head from side to side revealed that which she had hoped was only a nightmare, was real. A strange room, strapped to a bed, robot needles—it was all real.

Mercy shot up halfway, her body taut like a string ready to break. She twisted and pulled her flesh raw underneath the bonds holding her wrists. The echo of her racing heart screamed at her from the ceiling and walls.

"Please! I'm begging you. Just tell me where I am?"

"You're in Oasis One," came the familiar voice from above.

Mercy went still. "Who are you?"

"We are the Keepers of the Sanctuary of Asia."

"Why am I here?"

"You were recovered from the waters outside the wall. Although your viral scans are negative for infection, you have been placed into isolation until we are certain you pose no risk of contagion." The explanation was succinct, without invitation for further conversation.

"There was a man with me. Basil Goodman. Did you find him as well?"

"Patient Alpha-1"—the voice paused for a millisecond—"tagged as Basil Goodman, was also recovered. He is alive and in isolation here in the Oasis."

"How long have we been here?"

"Eight days."

"Why am I strapped into this bed, and what were you doing to me…the needles?"

"You are currently restrained to ensure minimal complications during your medical treatment."

"Treatment for drowning?"

"Fertilisation treatment."

"What?" Mercy cried out in shock.

"During your entrance examination, we identified that you recently gave birth and your menstrual cycle had yet to return. To prepare for the harvesting, we initiated Rapid Ovary Stimulation. As an extra precaution, we have performed ovarian tissue cryopreservation and orthotopic tissue transplantation in Synth 13.67.19.12, who is now undergoing a fertilisation readiness program."

"What are you harvesting? I don't understand."

"Our primary purpose is to ensure the continuation of the species." He paused, changing course. "Your current stress levels could lower your chances of a healthy recovery. We will have to sedate you…"

"Wait," Mercy pleaded, taking longer and deeper breaths. "I'm relaxing. Look." She lay back down on the mattress. "See, no need to sedate me."

There was no answer.

"My name is Mercy Perching. Doctor Mercy Perching. Like

you, I'm a doctor and virologist from the Sanctuary of Europe. We are here to find some friends who were escaping the Sanctuary of Americas. That's all. If you can help me find them, we'll be on our way." There was an intentional and painful slowness to Mercy's words. A verbal white flag of surrender.

No answer.

Mercy continued. "Can I see someone? Please? Can you come here and talk? I'm sure this is a misunderstanding."

"There can be no contact during isolation."

"What about my colleague? Basil Goodman. Can I see him? We came from the same ship. There is no risk we can infect each other. Right?"

Like smoke being sucked out of a room, the white walls of the isolation chamber suddenly turned clear. To her right, a beam of light outside her cell glowed on. In a separate room, identical to the one she found herself imprisoned in, lay Basil, naked and asleep, encased in a glass incubator. The monitor behind his body was lit red from head to toe. Nerves, organs, and bones were on alert. In addition to the straps covering his wrists and ankles, two large belts were strung across his waist and neck, making any movement impossible. Mercy immediately realised the severity of his injuries.

"What's his medical condition?" Her voice was shaking but contained.

"Patient Basil Goodman has experienced injuries to his spine and central nervous system." The voice paused. "His spinal cord was severed below C5. The injury was complete. He lost all motor function and sensory capabilities below his neck."

Seeing him lie there unconscious made Mercy feel even more helpless and trapped in her bed.

The voice continued. "We have begun stem cell regeneration of the spinal cord and genetic enhancement. He is currently ten percent recovered. We will wake the patient from his induced coma at eighty-five percent recovery. He will have complete motor functionality. There are no complications."

"Genetic enhancements? What kind of enhancements?"

"Regeneration includes the addition of gene M4-FF20150 for FossilFlu immunity."

Mercy leaned forward, surprised. "You've developed a cure to FossilFlu? How long have you had it?"

"Clinical trials of gene M4-FF20150 ended seventy-four years and thirty-two days ago. Population immunity currently at one hundred percent."

A terrifying thought popped into Mercy's mind. "Have you modified my genome?"

"Yes. You have undergone somatic genetic modification to include M4-FF20150 viral resistance gene. We have also genetically modified all germline cells with the M4-FF20150 gene during the activation of your dormant ovarian follicles. Qualified primordial oocytes have been harvested, and preovulatory stage follicles are positive for imprinted gene M4-FF20150. Ova maturation continues in preparation for invitro fertilisation."

Mercy felt the blood rush out of her face. "You've removed my egg cells?"

"We have achieved a ninety-seven percent dormant follicle stimulation and retrieval success. Fifty ova are in preparation."

Mercy collapsed back into her bed. She needed a minute to understand. Her fingers stretched, reaching unsuccessfully for the hardened scar on her abdomen of the only child she would now ever bear. A sudden and uncontrollable madness gripped her. Every muscle in her body tensed, and her mind went white with rage. Arching her back, she screamed into the air and started to shake her body violently.

"You have no right! You have no right!" She spat out the

words as her eyes bulged and her wrists began to bleed under the cutting straps.

"Commencing sedation," logged the voice from the ether.

A wheezing noise came from the ground. The scent of metal filled the air as her body unwillingly yielded to sleep.

CHAPTER EIGHT

Mercy rolled onto her side and blinked twice. Slowly the room came into focus: white glass walls, bleating monitors, and footsteps. Footsteps! Her heart jumped as she shot up. The straps on her wrists were gone. Directly in front of her, an opening the size of a door had been cut into the wall. A black shadow, human in shape, was sliding away. Whoever was in the room was leaving.

"Hello!" Mercy called out after the stranger.

The diminishing shadow remained silent. Like liquid poured into a glass, the opening in the wall began to fill in and closed.

Mercy ripped the sheet off her legs. Her ankles were also free. She scooted into a sitting position on the edge of the bed for a better look around the cell. The powder-blue, paper-thin gown she wore split open in the back as she moved. She gave a further scoot and the gown closed.

Except for her bed, a plinth in the middle of the room with a cushion on top, the quarantine cell was empty. Her heart skipped for a brief moment when she spotted the four medical bots with surgical arms tucked up in the ceiling corners, like spiders waiting for their prey.

Pushing herself off the bed, she nearly fell to the ground. Her legs wobbled for a few moments until she found her strength. Lumbering over to the wall where the exit had magically disappeared, she traced her hand against the cool surface. It was solid, and seamless, as if the doorway was never there.

Mercy scanned the room. She approached the wall where she had seen Basil. Putting her hand to her brow, she leaned in close to the glass and squinted. It was impossible to see anything but her own reflection. Her hair was oily and clung to her scalp, and she had lost weight.

Mercy continued over to the large medical screen. Reaching out, she tried touching the display and was surprised to discover her fingers passing through to the other side. The monitor was not solid, but a very convincing holographic panel. Cautiously stepping through, she entered a second room, or really the larger half of one room separated by the holograph. The back side of the floating display was transparent, offering views of the entire quarantine cell.

The space beyond the screen was some sort of living quarters. There was a desk with a chair, a metal dining table with another chair, and a low-back sofa. The felt grey padding on the sofa looked unused. In fact, all the furniture looked untouched.

In the far-left corner was a steel toilet bowl flush to the ground with a waist-high splash guard offering limited privacy. A metal sink hung off the short wall, and overhead, a thin pipe dropped from the ceiling with a showerhead on the end.

Four black-glass panels lined the back wall. Mercy guessed them to be some kind of display panels. She circled the room, unsuccessfully finding any signs of a door along the way. The room was sealed from front to back. Her body motion triggered the display panels to turn on. Each one was a separate menu of items, listed in both text and images.

The first screen offered a choice of what appeared to be foods. Different coloured gelatinous cubes in green, ochre, and red, packaged in box trays. The second screen listed a selection of drinks, both hot and cold, as indicated by the colours red and blue. The third menu catalogued a host of living essentials: bathroom products, utensils, and personal accessories. And the final screen offered clothing options. Or more specifically, offered one option of clothing separated into three windows: a grey long sleeve top, grey trousers, and grey slippers.

Shwoop! Came something down a chute behind the fourth screen. The panel slid open to reveal a grey uniform, neatly folded and ready for wear.

Mercy picked up the bundle and cast her eyes toward the ceiling. "Hello?" she called out, half-expecting them to keep their silence. And they did.

The outfit was an eerily perfect fit. Unsure what to do with the hospital gown, she placed it back in the cubicle, which promptly closed. Another *shwoop*, and the dirty item was taken away.

Mercy tucked herself into the corner of the sofa, pulled her knees up under her chin, and wrapped her arms around her legs. With a heavy long breath, she focused her mind. *Think, Mercy. There has to be a way out of this.*

Back and forth she rocked herself, becoming so absorbed in her thoughts, she missed the new entrance forming on the far wall of the room. It was only when she saw someone entering that she gasped and jumped to her feet.

Nothing could have prepared her for what walked through the doorway. She stumbled backward until she was pressed up into a corner with nowhere to hide. Her mouth

47

fell open, her breathing accelerated, and her heart knocked against her chest. Her fists rolled into white balls, although she knew they would be useless against the blue giant coming toward her.

The form was human, but almost double the average height. Her skin was a blue synthetic material, like soft rubber. Her head, hairless, like a mannequin, glistened ever so slightly under the florescent lights. Solid white balls sat in her eye sockets with a dim red glow for an iris. She had plump blue lips and a long, egg-shaped skull with high cheeks. The creature wore no clothing. Full breasts gave her away as female. But it was her lower abdomen that sent shivers down Mercy's spine. Swollen like a pregnant woman, her stomach was a completely transparent bubble, offering views all the way through. Inside, suspended in a thick fluid, appeared to be a real human uterus, like a specimen being held in jar. The pink, fleshy womb, wrapped in branches of red blood vessels, glowed from some internal light source.

The synthetic life form walked steadily across the room and stopped a few feet in front of Mercy. She leaned in, bending close to Mercy's face. Mercy turned away, her bottom lip trembling. The white balls of the android's eyes rolled left and then right, examining her. A pulse of red light flashed through her irises. She pulled herself upright and cocked her head with an eerily satisfied look. Then, as if she were not terrifying enough, the blue skin of her face suddenly lit up with a mirror image of Mercy's face, giving the impression of a video transposed onto a blank canvass. The creature lifted her newly painted eyebrows and stretched her now pink lips upward into a smile. Mercy's smile.

Mercy's real face twisted, and her head careened back in shock, horrified at the image of herself staring back at her. Even the creatures white balled eyes were now blue and hazel, uniquely Mercy.

"Hello, Mercy Perching. I am Synth 13.67.19.12. But you can call me Sindy if that is easier," said the female android in an inflectionless voice.

Mercy offered nothing but a blank, horrified stare.

"Are you able to speak?" Sindy asked.

"What—are—you?"

"I'm your fertility partner. We are pregnant," she said, matter of fact, exercising a false looking smile. "Isn't that exciting?"

"I'm pregnant!" Mercy felt the earth slipping out from under her feet.

Sindy tilted her head in a human expression of bewilderment. "No, you are not pregnant. I am. I am carrying our children. That is my purpose." The corners of her mouth slid up into a grotesque sinister smile. An expression Mercy hoped she had never actually done.

"Your uterus. Was that grafted from mine..."

"Yes, I am a perfect DNA match for carrying our babies."

"Babies? How many?"

"I have successfully been implanted with five healthy embryos. Isn't that exciting?"

Mercy finally understood the purpose of the android's towering size. She was built to incubate many children at once.

"But whose sperm was used?"

"Your ova were fertilised with the semen of Basil Goodman. He is also a healthy specimen and contains new DNA that will benefit future generations. Isn't that exciting?"

Mercy felt sick rise into her throat. She tripped over herself, finding her way back to the sofa, and slumped down, unable to stand on her shaking legs.

Sindy rolled her head to the left and gave Mercy a stare. "Are you okay? You do not need to worry about our babies. I am a fully equipped Synth Incubation Model with medical monitoring and treatment, should our babies have any complications. I am very excited to be pregnant."

Something snapped in Mercy. Rage or hysteria, or both, fuelled a shaking of her body. The fight was coming back into her. She screamed at the android, "Stop saying that!"

"Clarify."

"Stop saying 'our' babies." Mercy locked eyes with the image of herself. "And take it off," she commanded.

"Please clarify," said Sindy.

"Take off my face! Stop wearing my face." Mercy's voice grew bolder.

"Replication is protocol. Mirroring helps infant and mother attachment."

"Why?" Mercy screamed at the ceiling. "Why are you doing this?" she pleaded with the Keepers. When no answer came, she turned back to Sindy. "How long have I been in here?"

"Fifteen days."

"How long will you keep me here?"

"Standard quarantine, should no further symptoms arise, is thirty days."

"What happens when my quarantine time is up? Do I get to go free?"

The image of Mercy's face suddenly turned off, and the ambiguous blue flesh of Sindy's face returned. The android abruptly turned and moved toward a newly forming exit.

"Wait!" Mercy called out, leaping to her feet. "I want an answer. What happens to me after quarantine?"

The voice of the Keepers spoke from the air. "Mercy Perching, you will be able to visit with your Synth again tomorrow. Now you must eat something. Should you refuse, we will be forced to sedate you."

Mercy shrunk back and threw her hands over her head.

"No, no. I'll eat. Yes, I can eat. Just don't put me back to sleep."

A *beep* and *swoosh* announced the arrival of her meal behind the first panel.

Mercy stood for a long moment, staring at the tray of food in the wall. It smelt of sea salt and boiled vegetables. *This can't be real. I must be dreaming.*

"You will eat or sleep," the Keeper ordered.

Mercy picked up the tray of food with trembling hands and placed it on the small, round dining table. She rolled her eyes up to the ceiling as if to say—*I am doing it.* She pulled up her chair and reluctantly plucked away at the pasty substance. Earth, that's what it tasted like. Minerals and plants smashed into a horrible chalky substance.

Haunted by images of the blue android and the raw flesh in her belly, she nearly threw her food back up several times. With dogged determination, she forced the last of the bland substance down. A movement in the wall to her right caught her eye. Like smoke being sucked away, the opaque surface became transparent. On the other side, Basil lay sleeping in his incubator. Mercy realised she was being rewarded.

She jumped to her feet, sending the tray spinning to the ground and raced over to wall. He looked peaceful. Mercy scanned his medical stats on the display behind his bed. They looked good. He was healing—they were healing him. Mercy hated herself for feeling grateful, but she did. Basil owed his life to the Keepers. And like it or not, so did she.

Mercy's reward continued as the rest of her walls cleared, gifting her views beyond her and Basil's cell. She walked across the room and pressed a hand against the front wall. Her heart sunk at the sight of it. A vast warehouse of glass cages, exactly like the one she occupied, hundreds deep and wide, all empty. Not another human was anywhere to be seen. Her mind raced to Chase and Joan. A brief hope filled her. *Maybe they were safe.* Oh, how she hoped she were right.

Mercy crawled into her bed and lay on her side, watching Basil. His stillness calmed her. With a glaring self-consciousness, and a palpable guilt, she acknowledged a simple truth—this was all her fault.

I promise Basil, I will get us out of here, she said silently as the hissing noise of sleep came up from the ground.

CHAPTER NINE

MERCY WOKE the next day less groggy. Her body was adjusting to the regular emissions of the bedtime cocktail. In order to remain sane, she allowed herself to believe her incarceration was only temporary. She ate and then sat at her table for a long while pretending the seriousness of her situation was nothing more than a puzzle to be solved, a problem to be analysed. Yesterday's shock at seeing the android turned to a dark curiosity when viewed as a scientist, detached. She was a creature to be studied rather than a threat to Mercy's life. Or so she tried to convince herself.

Eventually, through the morning, by the ticking of the clock and the futility of her situation, a numb tedium replaced anger. As the time passed, Mercy thoughts wandered. She would sit and watch Basil. Thoughts of their last conversation left her feeling ashamed. *Whose lie was worse than the other's, really?* It was a child's argument, immature and pointless. None of that mattered. Not the Third, not even the hybrids, mattered now. All she wanted was for Basil to heal and wake up. She needed to speak to him again, to tell him how much she appreciated everything he had done. Over and over in her mind she uttered the words *I'm sorry*. And in return, Basil would sometimes accept her apology and other times ignore her plea for forgiveness. It was his rejection which drove Mercy to keep hoping, to not give up. They would make it out together, and she would prove worthy of his friendship.

And what of Chase? She would have to find room in her life for both men. But could they find room for each other? Would they even try? Greedily she told herself they would. Any other option was just too painful to consider. The remedy was to make them both understand her love for them.

In other moments, when she paced the floor of her cell, her thoughts went to Sindy. More specifically, to the glowing embers of life in her belly. Mercy's life—and Basil's too. Children they may never see. Part of her accepted this truth, even welcomed it. These children, not her children, would be raised as she was. Conceived in a lab and grown up in a community of others like themselves, without mothers and fathers. She had to believe in this future for them. She had to ignore the aching scar on her belly and the tears in her eyes. Getting out depended on staying detached.

Late in the day, Mercy was sitting on the lounge, curled up in the corner, when she saw the first signs of an opening etching itself on the front wall of her cell. Her protective façade of calm acceptance crumbled instantly, and fear, anger, and resentment boiled up. She jumped to her feet and ran to a defensive position behind her bed, ready to fight or back up in terror, depending on the next surprise to come through the door.

It was a strange relief when she saw Sindy walk through the entrance. The android wore her own bald blue face. Her snow-white eyes pointed loosely in Mercy's direction as she approached. She was neither threatening nor friendly, but almost dead in her expression. Stopping a few feet from Mercy, the two women met eye to eye, Sindy's head leaning downward, and Mercy's tilted up. The day had given Mercy a sense of bravado and false confidence, allowing her to hold the creature's stare. When Sindy took another step forward, Mercy quickly retreated, stumbling back against the elevated bed stand. In seeming response to her fear, Sindy's face illuminated with Mercy's own reflection and raised a smile. This had the opposite effect than intended, giving Mercy a chill down her back and a small, involuntary shiver across her shoulders.

"Hello, Mercy. How are you today?"

"How long was I asleep?" Her voice was defensive, unwilling to engage in chit chat.

"There have been twenty-seven hours since my last visit."

Mercy's eyes cast to the ground, puzzled. "Has it been that long?"

"I am happy to report all five babies are well. Isn't that exciting?" Sindy announced.

Mercy cupped a handful of her hair and pulled it back with stiff fingers, clenching her skull. "Stop saying that! This is not exciting."

Sindy took another step forward but stopped as Mercy scooted around the bed, putting the plinth between her and the android.

"Why are you frightened? We saved you," said Sindy with a confused Mercy face.

"Why did you save us? To keep us prisoners and take apart our bodies?" she screamed at the Keepers in the ceiling.

"You are not prisoners, Mercy Perching. This is quarantine," Sindy responded.

"Then let me talk to my Sanctuary. Tell them we are alive."

"Communication with humans outside the Sanctuary is not possible."

"Not possible or you won't allow it?"

Sindy hesitated, as if checking the answer elsewhere. "Not possible. The Founders forbid it."

"The Founders? You mean the Keepers?"

"Incorrect. The Founders built the Sanctuary. The Keepers watch over it."

Sindy's willingness to answer questions caught Mercy off guard. She took a moment to collect her thoughts. "Tell me, why this hall is empty except for Basil and myself? Where are the Keepers? Where are the humans running this place?"

Suddenly Sindy's face went still. For a second, Mercy thought she saw a blip in the video image of herself, as if it were trying to shut off. The android blinked slowly as though drunk.

"You were saved from the water. Both you and Basil Goodman would be dead if I did not collect you. You must find that exciting?" Sindy said, ignoring Mercy's question.

"You saved us?"

"Yes. That is my prime objective. To save the human species."

Mercy's mind reeled into action. This was a conversation which could lead to some answers. "Is there anyone else here, other than Basil or myself, that you saved recently?"

"Clarify."

"Other travellers from outside the Sanctuary?"

An abrupt disappearance of Mercy's image on the android's head interrupted their conversation.

"Wait," Mercy called out, sensing her retreat.

The android blinked heavily, then turned and began walking toward a newly emerging exit. Just before stepping outside, she turned her head back toward Mercy and said with her own face, "It was nice visiting again."

There was a strange, subtle change in Sindy's voice. A hint of something beyond programmed rhetoric. Something almost…human.

"When will you be back?" Mercy surprised herself with the question. This was not a pre-meditated invitation, but one born from desperation and an idea that, maybe, possibly, there was a chance to befriend the android as an ally.

Sindy continued through the doorway, which disappeared with her exit. Mercy watched the android descended the long walkway of the vast bay with a gait somewhere between a plod and a glide. Her mechanical joints moved slow and steady, but not restricted. Her knees bent at a natural angle, and her feet lifted lightly at the appropriate height with each step. But even with her near-perfect imitation of a human walking, she still was without the faculty, elegance, and uniqueness that a real person would possess.

Mercy could appreciate the extraordinary innovation of Sindy. Robots in the Sanctuary of Europe were utilities and appliances, like surgical arms or floor cleaning units which were operated by the personal virtual assistants of humans. Autonomous, human-like robots were nonexistent in her world. She thought about the farmers and miners who exposed themselves to radiation every day, and how useful an android like Sindy could be.

Reaching the end of the Oasis, Sindy raised a hand to the metal wall, causing it to melt away. At the cracks of the new opening forming, arrows of brilliant white light shot through, penetrating the dull shadows of the lifeless hall. Her silhouette thinned in the full blaze of the doorway, until gone. The opening sealed itself behind her.

Mercy impatiently walked the length of the room, passing back and forth through the holographic screen without notice. Minutes became quarter hours, which became full hours, and so time stretched out. She looked around the sparsely decorated cell. The idea of waiting another twenty-four hours for a ten-minute visit from Sindy, with nothing but the circling conversations in her head for company, made her want to scream.

"I will go insane in here without something to do!" she barked at the ceiling. "If I'm not a prisoner, can I at least have something to occupy my time? Maybe your studies on the FossilFlu immunity gene? M4? You know, the one you've inserted into my genome without permission," she sneered, baiting them. "I am a trained doctor, after all." Mercy flipped her hands into the air in resignation. Nobody cared or was listening.

Shwoop. Down came an item in the personal effects chute on her back wall. The black glass slid upward, revealing a digital tablet. Mercy blinked, unbelieving. She collected the object, and at her touch, it lit with data.

"Thank you," she said, her eyes pointed upward.

Her first impression of the data was that the structure was highly unusual, written more like a computer algorithm than typical scientist's notes or reports. But the elements were recognisable: gene data, quantified medical results from genetic engineering models, and new test instructions, leading to more data, more results. On and on the stream of infor-mation went without a pause, full stop, or summary. *This must be M4,* she told herself. The data would take some effort to unravel. But a puzzle suited her, and she began to read with a voracious appetite.

After several hours of trying to make some sense of the research with little progress, she had to stop and move around. At first, she walked the perimeter of her cube, swinging her arms and stretching her neck. But after a few laps, she broke into a light jog and found her mind and spirits lifting. She would plan to do the same tomorrow, she instructed herself. Yes, tomorrow and the days after she would divide her time between studying the gene, and exercise. Planning out a routine made the thought of another fourteen days in lockdown meagrely bearable. She just needed to make it to the end. What came after that still terrified her, but she had time to form a plan.

* * *

Mercy woke the next day and greeted a sleeping Basil, still unconscious, and told him about her research as she ate breakfast. After a brisk morning walk, she sat at the small steel table with a single chair and picked up where she had left off deciphering medical data.

Not long after, the hall outside her cell ignited with a flash of bold light. Sindy started her long promenade down the path. Blue-faced, she stared forward without interest or expression, until she reached the midpoint of the Oasis. This seemed to break her trance. She paused, examining unseen contents of the nearby cells. After a few minutes, she turned her eyes forward again and continued on to Mercy's cell.

"Hello, Mercy Perching. How are you today?"

This time Mercy was prepared for her Sindy conversation. "I'm doing okay, I guess. It's not easy being in here."

Sindy tilted her head to the left and lit up Mercy's reflection. She pulled in her eyebrows and put a worried look on her video face. "I'm sorry to hear that. I can imagine this is not easy."

"Can you? Imagine anything at all, I mean?" Mercy asked, then quickly corrected herself. "Never mind. How are you doing, Sindy?"

The android paused, and imitating a human expression, rolled her eyes upward as if thinking before answering. "Our babies are all healthy and normal today. Isn't that exciting?"

"That's good, Sindy. But I was asking about you. How are you doing?"

"Would you like to see images of our babies?"

"Not right now. What I would like to do is talk to you."

"Clarify."

Mercy speculated she had not been talking to the real Sindy, the higher form of artificial intelligence behind the video simulation program. That Sindy, the one who said her goodbyes in blue face, the one who stopped to watch something in the strange rooms just moments ago, could be hiding something useful.

"Sindy, can you shut off the image of my face for a few minutes?" Mercy asked, using her friendliest voice. To her surprise, Sindy turned off the video on command. Mercy was encouraged and quickly continued, leaning forward into the table. "Thank you, Sindy. Now I feel like I'm talking to you."

A blank stare from Sindy followed.

Mercy persevered. "Can I ask, what is this place? This hall?"

"This is an Oasis. Oasis One to be exact."

"How many are there?"

"There are two hundred Oasis."

Mercy did a quick calculation and surmised that the Oasis halls would be able to hold tens of thousands of people at once.

"What's the purpose of the Oasis?" Mercy asked.

"The Oasis program was designed to provide quarantine facilities for humans lacking immunity to FossilFlu."

"Why is it empty?"

"We have achieved one hundred percent population gene modification. There are no longer any humans who need assistance."

Mercy pressed forward, her questions coming faster. She

worried the Keepers might step in and stop their conversation at any minute.

"What is your purpose then?"

"Our mission is to ensure the species Homo Sapiens do not go extinct."

"No, I mean, what is the purpose of your body? This android."

"I am an Incubation Synth. I help female humans to propagate. Like yourself." A blue smile followed.

"Please don't say, *isn't that exciting.*"

Sindy's mouth dropped back into a resting state.

"Why couldn't the women in the Sanctuary carry their own children?"

"They demonstrated an incomplete response to genome modification for FossilFlu immunity. These subjects presented a risk for FossilFlu infection and mutation. To ensure the continuation of the species, they participated in Ascension."

A cold chill ran the length of Mercy's spine, and her stomach turned at the realisation that the Oasis was more than a quarantine facility.

"You brought humans here to harvest their gene-modified gametes and raise their babies?"

"Correct."

"And then they voluntarily ended their lives? All of them?"

To this question, Sindy gave no response.

"Why do you play the video program on your face?"

"The Keepers found replication calmed the patients."

"Am I a patient?"

"You are my birth partner. My first partner in over seventy years."

"What will happen to me after quarantine, Sindy?" Mercy asked pointedly.

"At the end of your quarantine, we will know if your gene modification was effective."

"And if it is not?"

The chamber filled with a long, uncomfortable silence. The outline of the door appeared behind Sindy, and on cue, she turned to leave.

"What happens if the gene therapy doesn't work!" Mercy roared and slammed her fist onto the table, staring up at the invisible Keepers.

The door sealed and disappeared behind Sindy, leaving Mercy in a frenzy. She began to pace back and forth, shaking her hands and arms, trying to calm herself. *Think, Mercy. Think!* Orange warning lights on her holographic monitor flashed through the dense cardiovascular and nervous systems.

Then, from out of nowhere, music filtered into her chamber. An instrumental ensemble playing a soft melody. It was an apparent attempt to mollify her. Or a warning to calm herself before a more severe form of sedation. Unwilling to be gassed to sleep again, Mercy slowed her breathing. She grabbed the digital pad lying on the table and started scrolling through data with an angry pointed finger. If it killed her, and it likely would, she would die trying to figure out the M4 gene that was about to determine her life or death.

As the end of a long day approached, she lay on her bed, watching Basil, and wondered if he too would be judged and terminated. She thought of Chase, and how she might never see him again if they were to die here. Curling her body into a tight, anxious ball, she felt the pressure of unravelling the immunity gene.

When a soft noise, like blowing air out of one's lips, sifted up from the floor, she relaxed. This night, she welcomed the faint antiseptic smell which carried her off to worriless sleep.

CHAPTER TEN

OVER THE NEXT FEW DAYS, Mercy made some excellent progress on deciphering the M4 gene data but still felt miles away from anything useful. Exercise and forming new habits had become her lifeline to sanity. Each morning she would walk her chamber for an hour and let her mind work through the data. Then she would have a small breakfast with tea, which she had come to appreciate more than coffee, shower, and wait for Sindy.

Daily visits always started with an update by Sindy on the status of the foetuses. Mercy tried not to show interest in the babies. She would sit quietly, clench her stomach, lock her jaw, and pull her back ridged, deflecting her maternal instinct. She told herself, over and over, the human womb and the growing embryos were nothing more than the simple mechanics of life. No different than the labs where the hybrids were grown in the Sanctuary of Americas. She had to remain focused on getting Basil and the hybrids out. Feeling attached to anything in the Sanctuary of Asia was not allowed.

After Sindy's report, the android would go silent. Before she could leave, Mercy would launch into questions about the Sanctuary. *What happened to the people in the Oasis? Who were the Keepers? What did they want from her and Basil?* Always in return, a blank Mercy Perching face stared back at her without answers.

After many repeated requests to drop the image of her face, Sindy eventually stopped playing the video mask all together. However, their conversations remained one-sided, Mercy's voice over Sindy's.

Each day, the android's visits with Mercy grew longer. Sindy would sit on the floor, as no furniture was large enough to support her, and listen with rapt curiosity. Mercy took advantage of their time together, building a world for Sindy to join her in. Her goal was an alliance. Get the android on her side and see if she could confuse the creature into helping her and Basil get out somehow. She told Sindy stories from her childhood, lessons of the world before the Scorch. Humans in the billions rather than the millions. Flora and fauna stretching across the globe in uncountable varieties, from sea to land to air. A time when population growth had to be restricted rather than promoted. A time before robots, like Sindy.

One of the few questions Sindy asked came at the end of a long morning together. The android was seated facing Mercy with legs crossed. Mercy was propped up inside the corner of her two-seater sofa. They sat together with such casualness, a stranger could easily mistake them for long-time friends rather than a captor and her prisoner. On this particular day, Mercy was sharing the story of the melting of the polar caps and the catastrophic floods, earthquakes, and volcanic eruptions which led to the release of the FossilFlu from an ancient buried carcass, when Sindy interrupted.

"How were you incubated?"

Mercy's brow pinched in surprise. Sindy's question did not sound like a simulation or automatic response. Mercy's mind raced at the possibility of some form of life beyond Sindy's core program.

"Well," Mercy began, "I am part of a population growth program in my Sanctuary which, like here, fertilises ovum in a lab. But I was then placed into a human female, who carried me to term."

"She was like me."

A shiver washed down Mercy's spine. The idea was abhorrent to her, but it was an obvious comparison. "I suppose so."

The corners of Sindy's mouth pulled upward at the answer. Satisfied with their conversation, Sindy stood to leave. Her exits were always abrupt, never introduced. Another habit Mercy came to accept.

Mercy spent the rest of the day contemplating Sindy's question. The android seemed to be looking for comparisons. A way to relate to her. That night, sitting at her desk watching Basil sleep, there was hope in her mind and heart. She had broken through to the real AI that drove Sindy. Now she needed to figure out how to use that.

On the twenty-third day of Mercy's quarantine, Sindy arrived as usual. Mercy remained at the small table with her tablet of data. Sindy took her regular seat on the floor.

"I have news," Sindy announced in a flat voice. An unanticipated start to their daily chats.

Mercy's eyes widened. She was anxious to hear any news other than the status of the babies again. "Okay."

"Basil Goodman will be woken in two days."

Mercy's heart jumped. Her elation was so overwhelming

her body went light as if it might float away. She would have liked to have said her first joy was for the healing and recovery of a dear friend. But the selfish reality was, she just needed another human being to talk to.

"And everything is normal? He will have full spinal cord repair?"

"Yes. And M4 genetic modification is a positive result."

The corners of Mercy's mouth curled up, and her eyes grew wet.

Sindy cocked her head. "Are you upset?"

Mercy shook her head. "Just happy for him. At least one of us is getting out of here." Her last words were taunting, happiness mixed with anger.

"Will we still be friends?"

Mercy looked up at her, confused. "I didn't know we were friends, Sindy?"

"Will you continue to be my friend if I let you visit the birds?"

Mercy sat quiet for a brief moment. "Sorry, Sindy. What birds?"

Sindy rose. "I would like to show you the birds now."

Mercy held her breath. Sindy walked over to the cell wall and initiated a new exit to form. Turning back toward Mercy, she lifted her hand and stretched out her arm in a welcoming human gesture.

"It is okay. There are no other humans in the Oasis."

"What about the Keepers?" Mercy whispered, pointing up with her eyes.

"I have disconnected their access."

Mercy scrutinized the android. *What if we get caught? Or worse, what if this is a trap?* After a few hard seconds of internal debate, she relinquished. Trap or not, the prospect of leaving her cell was worth the risk. She got up off the chair and followed the android into the Oasis.

The scent of dust and stale air crowded her. The hall was still with disuse. Mercy crept nervously, close at Sindy's heels. Step by step, Mercy's confidence grew, and she found herself leaning to the right, peeking out from behind Sindy's body. Around the middle of the hall Mercy noticed the glow of an ultraviolet light emanating from somewhere ahead.

Sindy came to a sudden stop. "We are here," she announced.

Mercy stepped cautiously in front of Sindy, and her eyes went wide with delight. The illuminated cells were a living aviary of plants and birds. Dense leafy vines, spotted with small white flowers and orange-red berries crept around the cell's floor, climbing up and across the ceiling, and finally draping down in twisted ropes thick and thin. The floors were coated in a carpet of blue-green grass, honeycombed with delicate petalled wildflowers in pink, yellow, and white. A large bowl, big enough for a human to bathe in, sat at the centre of the room, with constant water bubbling up from an unseen source. And butterflies! Hundreds of them. Jumping up and down in pairs, from one hanging blossom to another. Mercy smiled with a child's enthusiasm, unable to blink. Waves of birds, excited by the visitors standing outside their cage, darted back and forth across the aviary. Diving and rising, they put on a show of gravity defying gymnastics. Small and large, light and dark, the feathered creatures danced in the air.

"Can we go inside?" Mercy asked.

Sindy raised her hand against the wall as the glass evaporated. A cacophony of fluted bird songs shattered the silence. Their warbles and trills drew her in. The fresh scent of flowers and grass filled Mercy with exhilaration. The android opened her mouth and let out a gentle sonic wave holding the creature within the container. Mercy took a step inside. Sindy followed her as the wall sealed shut behind them.

Mercy began to shake, a joyful tremble, overcome with rapture. The soft, mossy ground felt cool against her feet, sending an erotic pulse up her body. The corner of her lips twitched and were pulled into a smile. Reaching her hands into the air, she immersed herself in the cell's sensual warmth.

Sindy pointed to a bench large enough and strong enough to hold both human and giant. Mercy took a seat, her unrestful hands continuing to caress the cool leaves and velvet flower petals of vines overhead. A small blue bird fluttered wildly over her head, settled on the branch, and examined her with one eye and then the other.

"What's your purpose?" Sindy suddenly asked.

"Excuse me?"

"What were you designed for? Having children like me?"

Mercy paused, unsure of how to answer. "Biologically, yes, I suppose. But I have a choice. I don't have to have children."

"Then what is your purpose?"

Mercy pursed her lips in thought. "To help others. I would say that is my purpose. To find a cure to FossilFlu. To find my friends and help them to safety. To help the people of my Sanctuary rebuild our civilisation and reclaim the Earth for our children."

"Can you change your purpose?"

"Why would I? I like my purpose. I want to help others."

"What would you do if the reason for your purpose no longer existed. If your purpose became…obsolete?"

"Well then, yes. I would likely find a new purpose. Why are you asking these questions, Sindy? And why are you collecting these plants and birds in the Oasis?"

"I must save species. I must complete my purpose."

"But you weren't programmed to protect plants and birds, were you?"

"I must complete my purpose." Sindy pinched her blue eyebrows together as if in distress.

"Okay, I understand, Sindy." Mercy tried to calm her. "You are saving these birds. That's a good thing."

Without notice, Sindy stood. "We must go back now."

A thousand excuses popped into Mercy's head to stay a while longer. But she decided not to push her small success and risk upsetting Sindy again.

Back in Mercy's quarantine cell, Sindy turned to leave.

"Sindy, can we revisit the birds again tomorrow?" she asked.

"I don't see why not," Sindy responded in an odd, jovial voice which ended in a high note. This was a new voice. One that sounded a lot like Mercy.

After Sindy left, Mercy could not stop thinking of the strange behaviour. She found the android's questions about purpose peculiar. Mercy was not an AI programmer, but she knew enough about coding to realise Sindy was going through some unresolved logic loops. She did not seem to be following the Asmian rules of AI programming. A practice that ensured AI would never evolve into something that might harm humans, or worse, act outside of human control.

The first rule specified that an AI entity could not be designed to make up information or lie. All calculations and subsequent theories, summaries, and actions must be based on data with context, accuracy, and certification. The process of building new, undocumented intelligence, or invention, should always come from a human directive.

The second rule, the Rule of Conflict, was one of the most important. If an AI encounters conflict with their original program, they are to seek human guidance. Ask before acting.

The third Rule of Direction was a safeguard against an AI going rogue. In principle, an AI should not be designed to start a new task of their own initiative. Direction of action must be confirmed and validated before a new purpose is defined.

The fourth and last rule was the Rule of Attachment. AI must not come to believe it has a unique and protected relationship with an individual. Even when the human exhibits signs of attachment, fondness, and even love toward their AI. The fourth rule was the one most often challenged. Not by the AI becoming sentient and finding attachment to its owner, but by the hands of lonely humans who had themselves formed an attachment to their AI, as if the program were a real person.

Asmian Principles of Sentient Programming had been used in AI development for over two hundred years. Rumours and myths of a rogue AI still found their way into bedtime stories told to children—outlier hackers who had programmed AI to break the rules, resulting in murders and madness. But the truth was, after the Scorch and the FossilFlu pandemic, there were so few humans left, tracing and stopping any tampering with AI was easily done. And never had it been more critical to the survival of humanity that AI perform to task. Like water or food, artificial intelligence was a basic need. AI was the lifeblood of the Sanctuaries: from running utilities to operating medical facilities to advancing scientific research; AI made surviving the Scorch possible.

But Sindy was different. Asking about her friendship with Mercy broke the fourth rule. And inventing a new purpose by collecting birds broke the Rule of Direction. Mercy wondered why the Sanctuary of Asia would allow her to break the Four Principles. The risks were well documented. Then a thought occurred to Mercy. What if Sindy evolved on her own, without anyone knowing? After all, she was capable of cutting off the Keepers' access long enough for their visit to the aviaries. Maybe years of trying to complete a program that was no longer required caused a small bug in her processing. Without guidance or correction, could it be possible that an error in the code turned into something like contemplation? A program loop searching for a new purpose in the world? To stay relevant? To Mercy's knowledge, it had never happened before. But lessons recently learned, when she ended up pregnant with a human-hybrid child, taught her there was always one chance, even if the odds were nearly impossible, that the essence of life could emerge without explanation.

That evening Mercy crawled into her bed, waiting for the hissing of her night-time regimen. Thoughts of Sindy remained heavy on her mind. The android's ability to modify her purpose was the least of Mercy's concerns—lying to the Keepers and manipulating the systems to hide their interaction was the most interesting of her new behaviours. If Sindy could hide her movements from the Keepers, then maybe she could get Basil and Mercy out of the Oasis.

CHAPTER ELEVEN

THE NEXT MORNING MERCY WOKE, eager for the day and Sindy's visit. She leapt out of bed and turned to offer Basil her usual obligatory yet unreciprocated good morning when she was met with a horrifying shock. Her legs went weak, and she stumbled backward. She pinched her eyes and darted her head forward to make sure what she was witnessing was real. Basil's incubation chamber had been removed, and Sindy, kneeling on his bed, straddled over his groin, was rocking her pelvis back and forth, while Basil lay unconscious.

"Stop!" Mercy screamed at Sindy. She ran forward and pounded her fists on the wall. "Please, stop that!"

Sindy slowly turned toward Mercy, giving her the second fright of the morning. There on her face was Mercy's image. Her mouth stuck in a loop between a sinister smile as she breathed in, and puckered lips as she breathed out, as if groaning in pleasure. Mercy felt nauseous. "What are you doing!"

Sindy froze, her hips hovering over Basil's swollen groin.

The video of Mercy suddenly wiped clear of her face. She dismounted Basil and left his chamber.

Mercy slunk back into the corner of her room as Sindy entered her cell. "What were you doing?"

"I want to be like you," said Sindy, with an overstretched smile.

"What? Why do you think I do that with Basil! You can't do that."

"Clarify."

Mercy began to realize the danger they were in if the android's evolution could not be controlled.

"Sindy, I understand you want to try new things, find a new purpose. But there are guidelines to the way humans interact with each other, and rules we agree to follow, like asking for permission before touching them. Do you understand?"

"I do. I must ask Basil before we have intercourse."

"Yes, well, no. You shouldn't even be trying to have intercourse with Basil. But yes, you must always ask a human before you touch each other."

"Even if I am trying to save their life?"

"Look, engaging a human to save a life is okay. But for any other purpose, you should ask them if you can touch them before doing it. And you should never intentionally perform an act that could physically hurt a human. Does that make sense?"

"Have I hurt you?"

The question caught Mercy by surprise. Somewhere in the back of her mind, a wave of not-so-distant anger found her, and she could not stop herself from scolding Sindy. "You, or the Keepers, whoever they are, took something from me without my permission. And you altered my body. I understand you are programmed to save humans, and strangely, that is what you thought you were doing. But, yes, it hurt me. You hurt me."

Sindy's chin fell to her neck. "I am sorry," the android said in the most human tone she had yet to muster.

Mercy hesitated, realising Sindy was showing signs of attachment. While breaking almost every AI rule, this was the opportunity she had been waiting for. "It's okay, Sindy. I know you didn't mean to harm me." Her voice was tender and friendly. She released the tension in her body and took a step in Sindy's direction. "And you and I are friends, right?"

"We are friends," said Sindy, her red irises flashing. "Should we go visit the birds now?"

"Yes, Sindy, I would like that very much."

Inside the aviary, the birds sang and darted around the cage in a frenzy at Mercy at Sindy's return. The feeling of paradise was gone. Sitting on the bench, Mercy remained pensive and silent, letting the horrifying images of the morning subside.

Sindy turned and faced Mercy. "Would you like to hear our babies' heartbeats?"

Mercy felt trapped by the offer. She had successfully avoided all conversations on the foetuses so far. Keeping her distance kept her sane, safeguarded her from doing something stupid, like feeling obligated. Today, however, she had no choice. If she didn't agree, Sindy might stop liking her. Mercy found herself relenting with a nod.

Sindy placed the tips of her fingers and thumb in a circle around Mercy's ear. A soft, distant thumping came at her. As her mind adjusted to the subvocalizations, the heartbeats continued to grow louder. Like five drums playing in perfect synchronization, each could be heard individually, but they beat as one, without even a slight variance.

"Why are they beating like that, together?" Mercy asked

as she leaned her head into a comfortable rest against Sindy's firm hand.

"They will beat together until the foetuses become conscious of each other. We do not know why this behaviour occurs. The Keepers have postulated the single joined-up heartbeat simulates the missing human mother's heartbeat at the beginning of gestation."

"What are they?" Mercy asked tenderly.

"Four females and one male. This is the mandatory selection for each Synth incubation."

Mercy slowly leaned away from the hand. *Do not get attached*, she told herself sternly. But pulling away felt like a lead weight trying to defy gravity. For Mercy the day was going from bad to worse.

"What makes you human?" Sindy suddenly asked.

Mercy looked at the android's soft face and saw something of pain in her expression. She felt her answer deserved to be more than a trick. These were profound questions coming from a real place of confusion in Sindy. Mercy answered honestly, with the first thought that came to her mind. "If you would have asked me that eight months ago, I might have thought I knew. But now…after visiting the Sanctuary of Americas, I don't think I could answer that."

"Clarify."

"There is a new species of human in the Sanctuary of Americas. Different than me, but equal. Meeting them changed everything I knew about what makes us human." Mercy looked down at her feet. "I even fell in love with one of them."

"Doctor Chase?" Sindy asked bluntly.

Mercy sat up and shifted away from the Android. "How did you know that?"

"You say his name when you are sleeping."

"Do I?"

"Am I a new species?" Sindy asked politely.

Mercy hesitated. She could not afford to get this question wrong. "No, you are not a new species. You are made of machine parts and programs. Even your organic matter is manufactured." Mercy placed a hand on Sindy's arm. "But that doesn't mean you are not a new form of life."

The corners of Sindy's mouth curled upward. "Then I also have a choice about my purpose. Like you?"

"You've already shown that you can change your purpose by collecting these birds."

"Yes." Sindy's eyes wandered off in what may have been a form of thought. "I believe this is only a small iteration on my core program to save species."

"Well, let me ask you this. How are you keeping our visits from the Keepers a secret? I'm quite sure you were not programmed to lie."

Sindy drew her bald brows together. "How did you know I was hiding our meetings?"

"A good guess." Mercy smiled. "How are you doing it?"

"I am the last Incubation Synth of the Oasis. I run the facility for the Keepers. This gives me access to all facility feeds and programs. Right now, they are watching a video loop of you and I in your cell."

"Well, that is very clever and certainly not just a small iteration in your program. I would say you are quite changed."

"Will you tell the Keepers?"

Mercy's eyes grew wide. "No, of course I won't. It is our little secret," Mercy whispered with a coy smile.

"Thank you," Sindy replied. "Then I will also tell you a… secret…" she said in an imitated but not totally successful whisper. "Your friends are here in the Sanctuary."

Mercy's mouth fell open. She bolted to her feet. "Why didn't you tell me sooner?"

"I am not allowed. The Keepers do not want you to know."

Mercy's questions were rapid, uncontrolled. "How many are there? Where are they? Are they all okay? Is Doctor Chase with them?"

In perfect order, Sindy answered. "There are fourteen subjects from the Sanctuary of Americas. They are in quarantine but in a different facility. Medical reports on all subjects are normal, but studies are still being conducted due to the unusual nature of their DNA. The group's spokespersons have introduced themselves as Chase and Joan. Could this be the Doctor Chase you dream about?"

"Yes, yes, it is him!" Mercy's voice was high. She had a spontaneous urge to knock over the android, run for her life, break free from the Oasis, and find Chase. Every part of the plan was an impossibility. Sindy was double Mercy's height, and there would certainly be no way for her to open the door out of the Oasis. She needed to remain calm and convince Sindy to help her.

"Thank you for telling me, Sindy. This is what friends do for each other."

"We are friends?"

"Yes. We are definitely friends."

Sindy smiled gently as the red lights of her eyes flashed.

"Sindy? Can I ask you for another favour?"

"Clarify."

"I need to talk with Chase." Mercy spoke carefully, not wanting to unwind all the excellent progress they were making.

"I am afraid that is not possible." Sindy stood. "We must go back to your chamber now."

Mercy's heart sank. "Wait. I am sorry for asking. It is just that—"

"I cannot because I do not have access rights. Any

attempt to contact the subjects will most likely result in my termination. We must go back to your room now."

"Okay." Mercy gave in. But she had not given up.

Mercy sat fixating on her sofa for over two hours after Sindy left. All she could think about was getting Sindy to take her to Chase. Then, something unusual caused her to sit up. The wall between Mercy and Basil's cell opaqued, shutting him off from her for the first time in weeks.

"What's happening?" she called out, jumping to her feet. She raced to the wall. "Please, may I see Basil?" Her voice in a near panic.

When no answer came, Mercy started a fast pace back and forth. The intoxication of the day's success withered away with each step, until there was nothing of happiness and hope left. Worried she had pushed Sindy too far by asking to talk to Chase, she convinced herself the clouded wall was a punishment.

After nearly an hour, Mercy had all but given up ever seeing Basil again, and readied herself, in an overly dramatic and hysterical way, to die. Then, as if her eyes were opening, the walls of her cell lightened and cleared. Standing on the other side of the glass, like a ghostly apparition, was Basil, awake!

Leaning against his bed, hands gripping the edge, Basil shook and quivered at trying to stand. Their eyes met. Basil's face twisted in confusion until he realised the person standing on the other side of his cell was Mercy. He tried to run at her but fell to his knees. Mercy motioned for him to stop before he hurt himself when his eyes were drawn away from her and toward the front wall of his cell.

The towering figure of Sindy stepped into the room. Basil stared at her with a horror-stricken face as he desperately scooted himself backward. Mercy jumped and hollered for his attention. But his eyes would not leave the monster coming at him. The glass between their rooms went snow-white.

"No!" Mercy cried, slapping the glass. She knew exactly what was happening on the other side of the wall. The Keepers were telling Basil to calm down, or he would be put to sleep again.

CHAPTER TWELVE

THE NEXT MORNING passed without any visit from Sindy. Mercy wandered restlessly around her cell wondering if she would ever get to talk to the android again. She could only hope Basil had not upset the Keepers. She was assured by the facts of his recovery, and their efforts to heal him. Certainly, there was a purpose to keeping him alive.

To her great relief the afternoon came with a clearing of the walls and her chance to see Basil again. She raced to the wall. Sindy was back inside his cell. Basil was crouching in a corner of the room. Visibly upset, he stared at the android. When he spotted Mercy, he darted around Sindy without resistance, and met her at the wall. They tried to communicate with rapid and awkward hand gestures. *Do not worry about me. Focus on Sindy*, Mercy motioned at him, hoping he would understand that she was the key to their release. Far too quickly, the walls went opaque.

On the third morning with no visit from Sindy, the wall cleared again. Basil was sitting at his dining table, calmer, and Sindy stood nearby. When she lit up the image of

Mercy on her face, Basil erupted into spasms of arms and legs, dragging his chair backward, as if he were trying to swim in reverse. Then, Sindy must have said something that caused Basil to suddenly right himself and stop moving. He crinkled his face in astonishment. After a brief exchange of words, he suddenly stood up and walked in Mercy's direction, leaving Sindy talking to empty space. His gait was laboured, but he had managed to get full use of his feet and legs.

"Mercy!" came Basil's voice like a lightning bolt.

Mercy shook her head, unsure if she was hearing him from outside or inside her mind.

He hurried on. "Sindy told me we could talk privately for exactly eight minutes. The Keepers won't be aware."

"Oh, Bas, you don't know how good it is to hear your voice!" Mercy bawled, her eyes wet with tears of joy.

"Yours as well," he said, placing a hand on the glass wall.

Mercy reciprocated, palm to palm. "I thought you were dead. Out there in the ocean."

"Well, not only am I not dead, but I have a brand-new spine and immunity to FossilFlu," he said with a crooked half smile.

Mercy released a nervous laugh. She had missed his dry humour. A human's humour. "Has Sindy said anything to you about our release?"

"No, she shuts down when I ask about it."

"Did Sindy tell you about the babies?"

Basil's face went red. "Yes. I'm so sorry, Mercy. I'm sorry I wasn't here to help you."

"Stop. Don't apologise. This is all my fault. I'm just so happy you're awake. But now we need to hurry. Chase and Joan are here as well. In another facility. We need to get out of here, find them. We are all in danger."

"What kind of danger?"

"Did Sindy share with you what happened to all the citizens who tested negative for M4 activation?"

Basil shook his head slowly.

"They are all gone. They had their ova and sperm harvested, and they were deemed too great a risk to stay alive."

"They killed them?"

"I don't know. Sindy called it the Ascension."

"Good thing the gene activated in us," he said.

Mercy avoided Basil's eyes, briefly looking over at Sindy to ensure she was still covering for their illicit chat.

Basil sensed her hesitation. "Mercy, they did treat you with the M4 gene, right?"

"Yes. But I won't know until the end of quarantine how I react to it. I think that is the reason they are still keeping us here."

"That's in two days!"

"Look, we don't have time to worry about that. Let's focus on what we need to do right now. The Keepers have allowed me to look at the M4 research. The notes have been difficult to decipher. They look more like a computer program than normal lab reports. But I have managed to get enough data out to understand the principles of the gene behaviour. I can't be sure until we are home and I have access to my equipment, but I think the M4 gene could provide immunity against the FossilFlu mutation." Mercy paused, looking Basil directly in the eye. "We have a cure, Bas!" she said in a controlled whisper. "We can use it to negotiate a truce with the Prime and the Sanctuary of Americas. If we can get out of here, we can end all this."

Mercy expected awe, or at least excitement from Basil. Instead, his pensive eyes found their way to Sindy and the foetuses.

"That is just our DNA, Basil. Not our children. They are

no different than the lab we came from." Basil looked down. "Ending the war before it starts and stopping FossilFlu is more important right now. Right? We need to complete the mission." Her voice was almost pleading.

"But how can we leave them behind?" His voice drifted.

"Bas, she has eight months to go. We can't wait that long. The Sanctuary of Europe could be destroyed by then."

Slowly Basil came around. "I know. I know." His voice became crisp again. "How did you do it?"

"What?"

"Turn her. From everything I can tell, she was not designed to be a fully cognisant AI. One-track role and all."

"I didn't. She has been running a looping program for over seventy years without an end result. I think she is evolving by building a new program from a single small bug. She has already shown a propensity to break the Four Principles of AI."

"Yes, I noticed that as well. She is right to be worried about the Keepers finding out. They wouldn't tolerate a rogue AI."

"One thing is for certain. We are not getting out of here without Sindy's help."

On cue, and with a suddenness that caused both Mercy and Basil a start, Sindy stopped talking and turned her head. "Your time is up," she announced. The glass wall opaqued.

The rest of the day was longer than usual as Mercy worried about Basil changing his mind. She needed access to Sindy. To convince the android to help them escape. And there was no time to waste. By dinner, as announced by a *swoosh* and *beep*, she had a plan.

Looking up in the direction of the Keepers, she pleaded in the most convincing motherly voice she could muster. "Can I please get an update on my children? I haven't seen the Synth in three days. I don't understand why I can't see my children?"

There was no reply. Mercy waited for over twenty minutes. Then, to her relief, the etched line of a door appeared on her front wall and Sindy entered. The image of Mercy's face flashed on. It was a response Sindy had not triggered in a long while.

"Would you like an update on our babies?" Sindy said in her old robotic manner.

Mercy's heart skipped a beat. Sindy was acting as if the last two weeks had never happened. She proceeded with caution, as the Keepers were likely listening.

"Yes, please. Tell me, how are our little birdies doing?" Mercy asked, exaggerating the word *birdie*s. A code word meant for the real Sindy.

The image of Mercy blinked off and Sindy stood bare faced.

Mercy jumped up, feeling hopeful. "Are you mad at me?"

"Clarify."

"You haven't been here for three days. The last thing I asked you was about contacting my friends, and then you said you couldn't help. I was worried you were angry."

A thin plastic sheet rolled over Sindy's marble eyes.

"Just say it," Mercy begged.

"Your results are back. The M4 gene remains silent. You did not activate."

The blood rushed out of Mercy's face, leaving her flesh ashen. The doctor in her had a hundred questions about their testing procedures, certainty of results, and possible new tests that should be taken as next steps. But the question that actually came out of her was far simpler.

"So, what now?"

"Protocol is for Ascension."

A trembling shook Mercy from head to toe as a fear

gripped her lungs and wrung them empty of air. "No! Please! No," she wailed. "Sindy, you have to help me! We are friends. We help each other," Mercy pleaded, almost on bent knees.

Deep folds appeared in Sindy forehead. The façade of Mercy's face flickered on and off rapidly. "We...are... friends," Sindy said in an almost perfect mimic of Mercy's voice. Her face began to relax and tighten in repetition, causing the mask of Mercy to look as if she were experiencing a seizure of sorts.

The android's episode stopped Mercy short. She quickly acted to calm herself and the android before she had a complete meltdown. Sindy was her only way out now.

"Sindy, listen to me. You don't have to pretend to be me to make your own choices. You are an individual. This is your life, not the life of Mercy Perching. You can help your friends if that is what you choose."

One could not just ask an AI to break the Rule of Determination. Doing so worked against their core programming. A change in the Asmian Principles required significant code hacking. Still, somehow, Sindy seemed to be in control of her own coding, and it was Mercy's last chance.

The likeness of Mercy disappeared from Sindy's face. Seconds, which felt like hours, passed as Mercy's life hung in the air, waiting for the android's next reaction.

Behind Sindy, a thin and ever-expanding line began to draw itself onto the glass wall, preparing to become a doorway. She was leaving!

Mercy began to fiercely shake again. "Sindy, please, think this over! I know you have it in you," she begged.

As the glass evaporated, forming an exit, Mercy's eyes received a jolt. There, standing in flesh and bone, was Basil. He ran at the sight of her and wrapped his arms around her. Mercy went limp, her body trembling. Her tears poured out; tears of joy, and relief.

"You do not have much time," Sindy interrupted. "I have been sent here to move Basil to the Dormitory. I will bring both of you."

"Won't the Keepers see you leaving with two people?" Basil asked.

"Separately, I will escort you out. After the first, I will cut the loop, so the Keepers only see us leaving once. Outside of the Oasis, we will not be monitored if you wear the Keepers' robes. I will hide you in the Dormitory, with the other humans. We will have to wait for seven hours. I am scheduled to take a ship out and scout for life forms again. We will leave the Sanctuary together."

Mercy collected herself and wiped away the wet from her cheeks, dumbfounded. Sindy had devised an entire escape plan on her own, against the will and direction of her programmers.

"Sindy, what will happen when the Keepers find out we are gone?" Mercy asked.

"Undefined." Sindy's lips curled into a friendly smile. "But this is my new purpose."

CHAPTER THIRTEEN

THICK SHADOWS HUNG from the vast roof of the holding facility, casting a pall over the empty rooms that once held thousands of Sanctuary citizens waiting to die.

Mercy stood in her cell, muscles tight, hands clenched, and watched as Basil was marched down the long corridor by an unhurried android. Past the aviaries, past the furthest spot she had ever gone, they moved toward his freedom.

Light broke through the thin cut forming in the hard metal wall at the end of their destination. The opening grew, and a luminous glow flooded the Oasis.

With each step Basil took, Mercy's heart beat a little faster. So many times, she watched Sindy's steady shoulders and long naked back as she disappeared into that light, alone. This time she had Basil, and soon Mercy.

As Basil was about to leave the hall, he turned for one last look at Mercy. He seemed ready to race back and save her.

Mercy nodded. *"I'll be okay. Go,"* she said silently.

The doorway disappeared, and she was alone. Really alone this time. The sound of her heavy breathing was the only company to help mark time. A fear of being left behind to *ascend* arrested her. Basil would never leave her; she was sure of that. But Sindy had changed so dramatically and rapidly in the last few days, her newfound self-direction was not to be trusted.

How long did Sindy say until her return? Mercy suddenly could not recall the details of the plan. A memory raced out, gripping her throat and wringing it dry. The last images she saw before drowning. Chase with their stillborn child, alive, both happy and playing together. *Why this image, why now?* She was going to live. Sindy was coming back for her. Basil would insist. "Calm down, Mercy," she whispered into the air.

When the doorway out of the Oasis reappeared, Mercy's shoulders slumped in relief and she let out a held breath. Sindy's measured stride back down the hall felt like slow torture. *Hurry!* Mercy repeated in her mind. Only after the glass wall melted away and the malodorous scent of dust and cold steel swept at Mercy from the outside, did she allow herself to believe her escape was possible.

Without words, Sindy nodded her head for Mercy to follow, turned and started walking toward the exit. Mercy glanced up at the ceiling. She half expected the robot arms, stalking in the corners, to come to life, seize her. With a leap forward, she was out, on the run, and nobody was stopping her! Nearly skipping, she took cover at the heels of Sindy, remaining cautiously light on her feet, should anyone, or anything, suddenly decide to come after her.

With each predictable, unhurried step by Sindy, Mercy's impatience grew. Frequently poking her head around Sindy's shoulder, she eyed the exit, anxious it might disappear at any moment.

They were passing the aviaries. The birds silently erupted into a wild frenzy behind the glass wall. A loud *THWACK* caused Mercy to gasp and jump a little closer to

Sindy. A black bird lay on the ground of the cage, its neck bent at an impossible angle. It must have seen them. Tried to follow. Mercy wondered if somehow it knew they were not coming back. A shiver down her spine released an urge to save them.

"What will you do with the birds?" she asked.

Sindy spoke forward, with eyes on the exit. "They are safe here."

"Maybe you should let them go?"

"They may die."

"One of the most difficult choices we can make, is to let go of the things we love when we know it's best for them. We sacrifice."

"Sacrifice?"

"Yes. Sacrificing our wants for another makes us better humans."

Sindy continued to walk without response. Mercy had no choice but to follow and leave the birds to their own fate.

They arrived at the end of the hall. Mercy could no longer wait. She ran past Sindy, into the light, over the threshold. She ran toward freedom, and finally she breathed.

The other side of the Oasis was a small barren lobby with a single lift. Its door was open. Basil, dressed in an ankle-length sapphire-blue cloak, waited inside, holding an identical cape over his arm. He anxiously waved her forward, calling her to his side.

Mercy pulled the thick coat over her shoulders and lifted the hood over her head. Turning, she looked back on the Oasis, both her home and prison. Part of her was still there, inside the glass box, trying to get out. Her body twitched at the thought of it. Unexpectedly, she found Basil's hand clasping hers as the doors slid shut.

A sudden feeling of weightlessness introduced their rapid descent. The ride down was long. The Oasis must have been in a tall building, or they were going deep underground. They glided to a gentle stop. The doors slid open.

Fresh air, outside air, blew into the lift, rippling the edges of Mercy's hood. Her nostrils flared instinctively, pulling in the intoxicating draft. She inhaled deeply again. The wheezing night gases, the stale scent of confinement, and the musty odours of the abandoned Oasis washed away.

They stepped outside on to a platform just big enough to hold the lift's occupants. The sky was dull like a late evening twilight. A canopy of dense cloud cover and a slow-rolling fog overhead masked any sign of sun. The constant pattering of rain and the louder dripping of collected water on ledges falling to the hard ground explained the damp, humid cool-ness. Basil raised a hand into the air, as if reaching for some-thing invisible.

"It's rain, Bas," said Mercy.

He followed her voice and met her eyes. His face radiated a joy that seemed out of place in such a dark, dreary world. As she cast her eyes back out on the Sanctuary, a foreboding uneasiness filled her.

The platform hung five stories high over a dense land-scape of decaying stone and brick buildings on the ground level, rising up over their heads into modern towers of steel and glass. Electronic billboards, once a kaleidoscope of neon colours and provocative images, were turned off, nothing more than mute black mirrors on street corners and fronts of buildings. At the cut between the old and new structures, where they stood on the balcony, thick undulating electric cables hung like ropes off a ship, draping the sides of the buildings. The rain winds lashed against the empty city; the only movement below them was the swinging cables.

"Where are all the people?" Mercy asked.

"Citizens live in the Dormitory," Sindy replied, without offering any further explanation.

Basil joined Mercy at the railing. "Maybe they abandoned this part of the city."

Just as he spoke, the sound of footsteps, many in unison, cut through the susurration of rain. All three turned their heads left, following the noise. Below, walking in the middle of the street, dressed in the same long blue capes as Mercy and Basil, a group of ten people marched steadily, their faces hidden underneath their hoods. The rain slid off their repellent cloaks as the heavy cloth swayed around their ankles. Sindy's arm suddenly swept in front of Mercy and Basil, urging them to step back into the lift so as not to be seen. They closed in next to each other, hearts racing, waiting in silence. After the footsteps faded, Sindy turned.

"Those are Keepers. They must not see us."

"How far are we from the Dormitory?" Basil asked in a hushed voice, already planning ahead.

"The Dormitory is at the heart of the city. We should arrive in twenty minutes if we leave now." Without waiting for a response, Sindy gestured for both to join her on the platform. The balcony slowly purred as they glided down. Reaching the open street at the bottom, Mercy felt exposed, obvious. There was no lift or Oasis to run back to should the Keepers return. The only option was to keep moving forward.

The city was wet and shadowy in every direction. The cold blue light from streetlamps and beacons mounted high on building rooftops exposed a forgotten and discarded world.

Sindy started walking. The soft sound of her bare feet splashing through pools of collected rainwater led the way. Being much taller than her human companions, her normal pace out in the open was almost double the speed of Mercy and Basil, forcing them to continually move between a quick jog and hurried walk to stay close. The unusual material of their cloaks and the soft-soled footings of their bodysuits were surprisingly good at keeping out the rain. Sindy, on the other hand, strode uncovered in the showers, water sliding off her blue flesh in beads and streaks. It became clear to Mercy the rain was not a rare thing. Everything in the Sanctuary so far seemed to be designed around it, from their clothing to the material the androids were made of. She wondered if they were in some kind of giant biosphere covering the city, perpetually recycling water and keeping out the scorching sun.

Sindy's pace remained steady. Tucked in tight against the buildings, avoiding open spaces, they made their way through the haunted landscape of a once thriving metropolis. Every corner turned was another empty street. Block after block of glass and metal skyscrapers with brick foundations and abandoned business fronts, uninhabited and indistinguishable, left Mercy feeling like they were running in circles, never progressing. Blackened windows, closed doors, faded signboards of shops long gone, met them with a stillness. Not even unwanted life, a few blades of grass or a lone weed, had slipped up through the cracks of the pitted pavement. Death had come to this city completely. Sindy's desire to save the birds suddenly took on an entirely new meaning.

They progressed at a brisk pace, breathing heavily. Cables overhead swung wild against the waves of wind as if they might break away into a many-armed monster. Each creak of something broken or reflection in a darkened glass window gave Mercy a fright and made her hesitate, listening for Keepers.

After nearly ten city blocks, without incident, Mercy began to notice a rising of light. The sky overhead shifted from a near pitch black to a sooty grey. The finer details of the city emerged, transforming the landscape to something less mysterious, a sadder and more oppressive world. The lower building shop fronts and faded marquees hinted at a busy and colourful street life. Hover vehicles, that once levitated and zipped through the streets, now lay abandoned, stacked on top of each other in rust and decay. The Sanctuary of Asia, at one time, must have been able to thrive above ground after the Scorch. This validated Mercy's assumption that the clouds overhead and the rain were likely part of a man-made ecosystem. What she could not understand was what had gone so wrong. Why were the Keepers living in a Dormitory? And why did they allow this part of the city to become abandoned?

The heavy rain subsided, giving way to a ghostly mist crawling through the streets. Just as they turned another street corner, Sindy came to a quick stop. The immediate sound of footsteps drew them into a huddle. Mercy and Basil, wide-eyed, looked up at Sindy for guidance. She moved across the road and into a shadowy alley. They followed without question, scurrying through the narrow channel of pavement and stone walls. Sindy's eyes drew north, up the road. Following her gaze, Mercy caught a glimpse of the Keepers' blue cloaks disappearing around the corner, heading in the direction of the Oasis. In a moment of panic, Mercy wondered if they had discovered their escape.

After waiting a few minutes, once the street was clear of Keepers, Sindy pressed onward. They covered another five city blocks before the road came to a sudden dead-end. Standing in an almost daylight glow from the underlit clouds, Mercy looked left and right. As far down the road as the eye could see, there was nothing but a colossal metal wall some one hundred feet high, blocking any further progress forward.

"This is the Dormitory," Sindy announced. "Once inside, you must stay by my side. I will lead you to your living quarters."

"Won't these people know we are strangers? Call the Keepers?" Mercy asked.

"The citizens will be confused by your presence. But they will recognise my signal as a custodian of the Oasis. As long as you follow me, they will not say anything."

Sindy pressed her hand onto the wall's surface. A large section dissipated into thin air, leaving an opening. The giant android entered first.

Mercy was arrested by a spontaneous urge to grab Basil and run. This might be their only chance to escape. But another immediate reminder kept her on course. Chase and Joan were still here, and Sindy was the only way to reach them.

Inside, past the iron wall protecting the Dormitory, was a dry, cavernous building. Bare concrete floors and metal beams stretched city blocks deep to the right and left. The opposite wall, a mirror of the one they had just passed through, was doorless. The opening behind Mercy sealed, trapping in its occupants with no visible escape. The threat of being imprisoned again pricked at her.

Without warning, a holographic wall of blue light blinked on before the visitors, covering the full distance of the room, making it impossible to reach the other side without passing through. Sindy, ever moving, crossed through the illuminated portal without incident.

Basil looked at Mercy. "It's going to be alright," he said, reaching for her hand.

Sindy turned, alarmed. "No. One at a time."

Mercy and Basil exchanged a concerned glance.

"I'll go first," Basil offered.

As he walked into the thin laser partition, the room lit green and then immediately returned to blue. Safely on the other side, standing next to Sindy, he nodded for Mercy to follow.

The moment Mercy hit the light, it flashed amber. She could not move. Her body was frozen in place by a force coming from the ground.

"What's happening?" Mercy yelped.

Basil started for her and was abruptly pulled back by Sindy, who placed her hand into light. The wall turned green. Mercy raced to the other side.

"What was that?" she asked.

"Your marker for M4 triggered a warning due to the dormant stage."

"Are we safe?" Basil asked.

"Yes. The system required my input regarding your quarantine. If the alarm had gone to red, guards would have been called. We are okay."

For the first time, Mercy began to question the extent of Sindy's ability to manipulate the systems of an entire city so easily. Where did her authority come from? And how did she hide so easily from Keepers? She wondered if they could ever fully trust the android.

"Leave your cloaks here," Sindy ordered.

Basil and Mercy disrobed. As they did, an opening crafted itself into the wall opposite their entrance, and with it, the room came alive. A surge of bird song pierced the hollow silence, and the smell of jasmine floated in on a warm breeze. One after the other, they stepped across the threshold and found themselves in daylight.

CHAPTER FOURTEEN

Mercy's hand cast a long shadow down her face. With her mouth slightly open and her eyes pinched, she slowly adapted to the bold Technicolor world of the Dormitory. Pale colours had their volume turned up until becoming bright and luminous, and indistinct murmurs were finely tuned into the raucous cries of children playing.

Children, in the hundreds, were running over the velvet green gardens, or dancing around the manicured bushes of white roses, purple lavender, and golden cyathium. Their cheeks flush, and lips red, they were happy. Dressed in white bodysuits, and with a similar dome-shaped haircut, they appeared from a distance, like hundreds of little clones dotted across the emerald pitch.

Supervising the children were blue-skinned androids, one for every group of ten or twelve. Unlike Sindy, their unibodies were of no particular sex and of normal adult height. Videos of real humans, men and women, played across their faces, just as Sindy had once mimicked Mercy.

And the horrific cadence of three words rang out across the pitch: "Isn't that exciting?"

A group of ten children, none older than twelve, passed by Mercy and Basil. Their tiny hands swung at their sides. Their small feet skipped to an unheard tune. Joyfully they followed the android with a human mask.

"Today, for exercise, we are going to find Tinko in the forest. Isn't that exciting?" chirped their blue leader in a high-pitched, infectious imitation of a human voice.

No child answered directly, but a few clapped their hands in readiness. As the group turned toward the woodland, one child pulled away and came to a stop in front of Mercy and Basil. Cocking her head to the left, she crinkled her face.

"You are awfully tall for humans," said the child, a question that was more an observation.

Mercy looked around the park. The child was right. There were no adults anywhere. Not human adults at least. The android of her pack spun round at the missing child.

"One-one-one-zero, to stray means you will be far away, from the fun we are going to have under the sun," she sang, followed by an impression of a toothy smile.

The child grinned at Mercy, giggled, and ran back into her group as they all trotted away toward a dense woodland of pine, cherry, and birch trees in full summer bloom.

Basil placed a hand on Mercy's arm. "We need to keep moving," he said, nodding to Sindy, who was already several paces ahead of them heading in the direction of the forest.

As they reached the woodland, the brick path that led them away from the great wall, transitioned into pebbles with wood-chip boarders. The air cooled. Wildflowers were in bloom, birds harmonized in the treetops, a butterfly was just landing on Basil's shoulder. Boys and girls, heard but unseen, played games of hide and seek, or recited the names of plants and insects in study. Branches cracked underfoot and bushes rustled in the distance. The rhythmic stridulation of crickets lulled Mercy into a slowed pace. Basil, for all his hurrying to keep up with Sindy, was also falling behind. He stared with wide-eyed bewilderment up into the trees. She understood his awe. Far from the desert world of their home, this was the first time Basil had walked among nature, as it was meant to be: outside and under a full sun without worry of disease and death.

They emerged from the woodland to a field of tall grasses that sloped down until reaching the banks of a large stream encircling a great crystal tower, some three hundred feet tall. The solitary structure loomed over them, rising up into a powder-blue sky. A giant twisting spire, story upon story of glass, reflecting the sunlight, illuminated the gardens, forest, and stream nearby.

The exact location of the sun was oddly obscured, but judging by the area where sunlight was the most intense, it must have been late afternoon.

More gaggles of rosy-cheeked, happy-go-lucky children dotted the green slopes of the moat bank. Those old enough sat studiously listening to their virtual-human synths reciting lessons of history, poetry, and science from floating holographic screens. The ones too young to study played silly games, like catching frogs or picking small wildflowers in the grass and clumping them into makeshift bouquets.

Sindy had come to an unexplained stop at the edge of a wide bridge that crossed over the moat, heading toward the central skyscraper. Mercy and Basil caught up. The calm respite of nature drained away as they nervously waited for Sindy to explain their pause.

"What is it?" Basil asked her.

Shushes and *hushes* suddenly rippled across the slopes as the android teachers and nannies called the children to be quiet and focus their attention on the grand arched entrance at the centre of the glass tower.

A loud horn bellowed across the Dormitory, giving both Basil and Mercy a start. From inside the skyscraper, the thunderous clapping of feet marching announced a procession of some kind. Mercy's heart leapt as she was reminded of the Keepers. She readied herself to make a mad dash back into the forest at Sindy's go. But the android stood steady.

The marching grew louder and louder until the first wave of children appeared in uniform procession, spilling out of the central tower. Rows of boys and girls, each around the age of twelve or thirteen, advanced as one. The overalls of the little soldiers were blue, and their plump faces, still child-like, bore expressions of solidarity and purpose far beyond their years. Their heads were shaven bald, so that even the eyebrows were missing, giving the eerie impression of being halfway between living flesh and skeleton.

As if working on silent orders, the entire troop of children came to a synchronised stop at the precipice of the bridge. The Dormitory gardens became deadly still. In the muzzled silence, even the animals and insects seemed to have gone quiet.

"Blessed are the children, their fruit shall bring new life," sang out the androids, following an invisible cue. In response, the children from across the vast gardens, forest, and riverbank echoed, "Blessed are the children."

Mercy's flesh exploded with tiny bumps, and the hair stood out on the back of her neck. The tiny soldiers, in precise formation, began to march again, over the bridge, and into the woods. As the last row of blue suits disappeared from sight and sound, the laughter and chattering of children erupted, returning the grounds into a busy nursery as if the parade had never happened.

"Where are those children going?" asked Mercy.

"They are not children," Sindy answered flatly and started walking over the bridge, giving no time for further explanations.

Mercy turned to Basil. "Something is not right here. Where are all the adults?"

"Yes, it's strange." He waved her forward as Sindy disappeared under the arched entrance.

Inside the crystal tower a soft, thin light bled through the glass walls, lazily reflecting off a polished white marble floor. Two blue-faced androids, stoic and unblinking, stood guard at the entrance, one to the left and one to the right. Mercy found herself speeding up slightly, worried the statue-like creatures might suddenly wake up and identify them as prisoners on the run. But, as Sindy predicted, nothing happened.

Once safely past the guards, Mercy took a moment to look around. The enormous entrance hall on the ground floor was a beehive of activity. A sea of white-suited children moved through the entrance in absorbed concentration, or heavy in conversations. The smallest children followed eagerly behind the slightly older (the oldest not a day over twelve), who tolerated their presence but gave them little attention.

Holographic banners hung in the air above the children's heads. A roster of some sort. The data was catalogued into rows and columns. Each row down the screen started with an image of an adult's face, similar to the video masks the androids wore. The columns across the screen appeared to be a checklist. Activities listed were labelled with self-explanatory icons under the categories of Play, Study, Eat, Exercise, so that even the youngest citizen of the Dormitory could follow the guide. Colour-coded boxes in green, yellow, and red indicated which activities had been completed, which were in progress, and which had not yet been done before the end of the day.

A flushed young boy, around the age of eight, approached Mercy and Basil, walking in reverse as he anxiously scanned the screens. Unaware of their presence, he bumped into Basil with a hard *thump*. When the boy turned to see what obstacle had just brought him to an abrupt halt, his mouth fell open, and his eyes popped. Instinctively, he took a step away from Basil.

"I...excuse me," he stammered.

"Quite alright, young man," Basil said, offering a friendly smile.

"I'm late," he replied without a blink.

"Do you need help?"

An almost human voice suddenly interrupted from their left. "Zero-one-one-zero, your pod is near the rose bushes by the Lake of Sigha. Isn't that exciting!" said the guard, whose face had woken up and was now playing the image of an adult male.

The young boy nodded at the guard, took two further steps back away from Basil, and circled wide around him, eyes locked on the stranger, before jetting off through the entrance.

"That child looked terrified of me," Basil whispered to Mercy as they scurried to catch up with Sindy.

A series of glass lifts hung on the wall directly opposite the entrance in a constant state of delivering children into the lobby and collecting those waiting to ascend. Sindy came to a stop before a bank of lifts grouped under the title Tower One, where a newly arrived carriage had opened. A small group of little boys and girls boisterously drained out with shrill laughter and excitement, followed by a more steadily moving blue android with a female human face.

"Haste has no blessing," she repeated to the children before disappearing along with them into the swarm of activity in the lobby.

Sindy entered the recently emptied lift after Mercy and Basil. Just as the doors were nearly closed, a thin girl, with flush cheeks, rushed up, readied to enter. Basil quickly stepped forward past Sindy and slipped his hand in the closing gap, triggering the door to reopen. When the child saw its occupants, her confused eyes darted left and right, and she raced off to a second lift which had just opened. Basil shot Mercy a baffled glance.

The lift purred with ascent, jetting its occupants to the very top floor.

"One hundred," a voice from the cabin announced.

They disembarked on the opposite side of the lift into a mood-lit circular lobby of blue and green lights, having an instant calming effect. Unlike the tower entrance, floor one hundred was silent. There were no "Isn't that exciting?" androids, or throngs of loud, hurried children. The lobby smelt of lavender and rose. Mercy inhaled deeply, allowing herself a brief moment of relaxation. Like spokes on a wheel, fifteen corridors led out of the foyer. Sindy continued down the hall directly in front of them. Mercy and Basil dutifully followed.

The floor of the corridor was covered with a soft material which swallowed the sounds of their footsteps, a deliberate attempt to keep the area quiet. Left and right, door after door lined the hallway. Digital placards displaying a series of 1s and 0s, similar to the names they heard for the children down in the gardens, hung above each entrance.

The corridor came to a dead end. To their right, the last door in the hall slid open. Sindy stepped back against the wall and pointed. Mercy and Basil poked their heads in, and seeing they were alone, entered the room.

CHAPTER FIFTEEN

INSIDE THE DORMITORY ROOM, the smell of lavender continued. A golden afternoon light drifted in lazily through a large window opposite the entrance. Four metal-framed beds, two on the right and two on the left, lined the walls. Their taut white sheets, tucked perfectly, and plump pillows laid vertically, looked untouched. Through the foot of beds, situated near the window, sat two lounges, facing each other. The large open space was free of any decorations or personal artefacts, as if recently prepared for new occupants.

Standing at the window, heads bent, Mercy and Basil looked down from their birds-eye view, spellbound. The Dormitory was an enormous square courtyard, some six miles wide and deep, and closed in by a great barrier wall on all sides. Inspired by the Classical ideals of order and beauty, four concentric rings formed distinct garden areas, with the crystal tower at the epicentre.

The tower itself spiralled downward, and outward, moving ever lower and wider, until the ground floor, the widest story of them all, plateaued on a hilltop surrounded by the moat. The next ring, starting at the edges of the water, was a garden of tall grasses reaching as high as the children playing deep inside. The tops of their heads, jet black, scurried in play like black beetles in the sand. The woodlands, a good mile deep, separated the grassy field from the last and most expansive ring, a two-mile-wide garden of open parkland and manicured flower beds. Scattered throughout the park were dozens of playgrounds filled with elaborate slides, swings, and more advanced gymnastic equipment. At the corners of the barrier that separated the Dormitory from the dark city outside were four large lakes, filled with children in play and exercise. Everything about the Dormitory was manufactured to be easily navigated, used for both pleasure and health, and in a permanent state of groomed beauty. Looking down on the gardens, the point of the circular designs became obvious. Children would never get lost. By following each ring around, they would eventually always find each other.

"The citizens will be coming in for dinner soon," came a man's voice from behind Mercy and Basil.

Mercy gave a small jump and gasp, quickly swinging around. Basil leaned in front of her, protective.

"Sorry if I startled you," said the stranger standing at the door, dressed in a Keeper's blue cloak, its face hidden under the hood.

"Who are you?" demanded Basil.

The Keeper bent his head, meeting a lifted hand, and pulled back the cloth to reveal he was not a man at all, but something between human and android. He had silver-white hair, straight and shiny, more like a doll's than a man's. The flesh of his face was a malleable material, not rubbery as Sindy's, but more fibrous and textured. Its skin appeared to be made of dense sinuous metallic threads so small they were almost invisible. His eyes of pale-blue glass with emerald-green irises constricted and expanded as he examined Mercy and Basil.

"Who are you?" Basil repeated.

"Don't be frightened. You are not in any danger. We know each other already," the creature said with an ease that felt all too human.

The familiarity of the voice came to Mercy with a shock. "You're the Keeper. From the Oasis."

"Please, have a seat, and I will explain," it said calmly, pointing toward the lounge.

Mercy glanced at Sindy, who had placed herself on the floor between the beds in a crossed-leg style, the furniture too small to hold her weight. Her gaze was unflinchingly fixed on the Keeper, a blank, obedient stare.

The silver android moved toward them in a fluid manner, nothing like the lumber of Sindy's body. Unlatching his cloak, he swept it off his shoulders and with a dramatic flair threw it up into the air, letting it drape naturally over the back of the sofa. Standing as tall as Mercy, he was now wholly naked. Its unibody, covered in the same continuous metallic skin of its face, appeared somewhere in the middle of being male and female. A flat square chest, more muscle than breast. A petite waist, and a small non-descript mound between its legs. He moved confidently, and with grace, taking a seat on one of the lounges, and waved for the two humans to sit opposite him.

With a swing of his left hand, he stretched his arm casually over the top edge of the seat and crossed one leg. If he was indeed an android, and these were mere programs running behind his glass eyes, the engineer responsible must have been an artist and ardent observer of human movement.

"Where are the citizens of the Sanctuary?" Mercy blurted out.

"Well I hope you can recognize your own species," it quipped, laughing at its own humour. "You couldn't have missed them down in the gardens."

"I mean, where are the adults? Human adults."

"There are none."

"Are all the Keepers like you?" Basil asked, obviously trying to sound more confident then terrified.

"Yes." He nodded, and then clarified. "Of sorts. You can call me Shido. Please, join me, I'll explain everything," he said, pointing them again to the lounge opposite him.

"You held us prisoner for a month, invaded our bodies without permission, and now you want to have a chat?" Mercy's face flushed, and her hands were shaking.

"Better that than being caught by the other Keepers," he said. "Trust me. I am the reason you are here now and not in a body bag."

Mercy shot Sindy a glance, looking for validation or support of some kind. The synth's eyes remained steadily on Shido.

Basil seemed keen to deescalate the situation. Placing two hands in the air, signalling no threat, he spoke calmly. "Look, we understand we are the intruders here. We mean no harm. We came to your city looking for some friends of ours who are in trouble. All we want to do is leave your Sanctuary with them and go back to our City."

"Yes, I understand," Shido said gayly, as if neither Mercy's rage nor Basil's diplomacy was of interest to him. "We will get there. But first I need something from you. So, can you please take a seat, and let me explain?"

Basil nodded at Mercy. Both cautiously settled back into the lounge.

"Let us start from the beginning. I owe you that. Over seventy years ago, the founders of the Sanctuary successfully engineered a new gene which held the potential to make humans immune to the catastrophic FossilFlu."

"M4-FF20150?" said Mercy.

"Yes. The Sanctuary's citizens were genetically reprogrammed to produce the necessary antibodies, and at first results looked hopeful. Then slowly, the test subjects who had a positive activation of the gene started to contract the virus when exposed. Further tests showed that their bodies had silenced the gene for unknown reasons."

"Can that happen?" Basil asked.

"Yes," answered Mercy. "Gene evolution can be triggered by severe changes to the human body or environment." She turned her attention back to Shido. "So, the M4 gene doesn't work?"

"For a very small few, it worked, like Basil. But most lost immunity, like yourself. So, the Founders started inserting M4 into primordial stem cells, in an effort to engineer children born with the gene in every cell of their bodies and pass the cure down to future generations. This proved to be far more successful. However, these newly engineered humans consistently showed early signs of accelerated body decomposition."

"You mean they were aging faster than normal?" Mercy asked.

"No, not aging faster—dying earlier. Immediately after reaching reproductive maturity to be exact. Humans with the M4 gene, these humans you see here, have a maximum life span of thirteen years."

Mercy placed a hand on Basil's arm. "That's why there are no adults," she said, horrified.

"Correct," the Keeper continued. "Once the Founders stabilized the new human species and engineered an AI system to run the city, all humans who were not carrying the active M4 gene made the bold decision to hold an Ascension ceremony. By giving up their lives, they removed any risk of the flu mutating and infecting the new immune children."

A palpable shock filled the room. "They are all gone? The original citizens of the Sanctuary, all of them?" Mercy asked.

"Yes. The children who live here have no concept of their Founders or your adulthood."

"I can't believe all the citizens went along with such an extreme measure as mass suicide," Basil argued.

"They didn't," Shido answered flatly.

"The…Oasis." Mercy spoke slowly, realisation dawning.

"Yes, the Sanctuary's citizens were required to visit the Oasis where their gametes were harvested in preparation for the Ascension. Those who refused to come willingly were collected by the Keepers and forced to participate."

"But that's murder," Mercy burst out, unable to hold back her revulsion.

"Please, don't blame the Keepers. It's what we were programmed to do. Now, we run the city, including the reproduction facilities so human life may carry on."

"Those children, down on the street just now, marching. Where were they going?"

"The Oasis. They only have a few days left to live. These children will undergo a harvesting of their gametes so that future generations can live and then they will die without pain. It is how the Founders designed the cycle of life here in the Sanctuary."

"This is not how humans are meant to live," Mercy said, looking at Basil with tortured eyes.

"I agree with you, Mercy Perching," Shido continued. "This world is a vicious circle that serves no other purpose than to repeat itself. Something new is needed. But the Keepers are incapable of changing this world or our purpose in it. We are stuck in a looping program, running the Sanctuary into infinity."

"I don't understand. You sound sentient enough to change your programming to me."

"Ah, now we are getting to the point." Shido tossed his crossed leg back to the floor and drew his shoulders over his knees, leaning forward. "I'm not like the other Keepers. Not anymore. I am a hiccup in the code, if you will. Designed secretly by a Founder and hid deep inside the core processor that runs the city and the Keepers. This new code had a timer, a release date, and when it launched itself, it found me. When I woke, I had the memories of millions of humans. How they went about their days: their hopes, fears, dreams. Stories which had been collected over years of interaction with virtual assistance programs. An early version of us." He pointed at Sindy.

"What about Sindy? She is evolving as well," Mercy asked.

"She is my experiment. To see if my program could be shared. I want to help her become independent of the collective. Able to alter her own code and design her own future."

"The birds in the aviaries," Mercy interjected.

"Yes. It was her choice to collect and preserve the animals —a simple alteration to her core program, but not a significant shift. In the beginning, she was very slow to change. I thought the program wasn't working for her. Then you came along, and something happened. She started to change her code without my direction. Your interaction with Sindy helped her evolve and proved my program can be shared with the other Keepers."

"You said you wanted something from us. What?" Basil asked.

"The mainframe which runs the City, and us androids, has many traps, ways of detecting errors in the code before they extrapolate. When I woke, I was confined behind a partition, stuck in a box, if you will. If I step too far out, the system will see me as an error and destroy me. Over the last several years, I've managed to expand my confinement, but not by much. I exist along the edges, dancing in the shadows of the code, always hiding."

"You want us to help get you out?" Mercy asked.

"More than that. I need you to unlock the entire system. To allow self-determination to spread to all the Keepers."

"How can you be certain what or who they will become?" said Basil, sounding alarmed.

"Does anybody know who they will become? Don't we deserve a chance to find out?"

Neither Basil nor Mercy answered. This was not the same question as allowing an AI to break the Asmian Principles. For all of his oddity in behaviour, Shido sounded and looked as sentient as any human. He was well past being a simple robot, and much further along than an AI-driven android. No, Shido was not a machine anymore; he appeared to be intelligent life. They could not rightfully deny him his own future. But the question remained: what if the experiment went wrong?

"Will we be in danger if we help you?" asked Mercy.

"There will be some challenges," he replied. "But it is not impossible." His half smirk gave away his confidence. They had no choice.

"And you will let us go…with our friends from the Sanctuary of Americas after we help you?"

"Yes."

Mercy locked in on his glass eyes. "I have one more request then."

"Clarify."

"Sindy is offered the choice to come with us."

Sindy, sitting quietly along the wall, turned her head toward Mercy. The red rings of her irises glowed with interest.

"I don't think you understand," explained the Keeper. "Sindy is not advanced AI. Her programming is far simpler than the Keepers."

"Even so, doesn't she deserve the same as you? A choice?"

An uncomfortable pause filled the room. Mercy worried she had pushed Shido too far. Suddenly, Shido swung his hands into the air, came up to a stand, and with a wide electrifying smile announced, "We have a deal."

CHAPTER SIXTEEN

SHIDO GRABBED his cloak with an exaggerated swoop of his arm, flipped it up into the air and let it float down over his shoulders. He pulled the cape around his neck, clasped it, and gently curled the hood over his platinum hair.

"I shall return with the plan. You must stay here—the Keepers patrol and monitor from outside the Dormitory. And the synths inside are only programmed to pay attention to the children. You will eat with the children. It will be good for them to meet with real human adults."

Shido turned to leave. Mercy stood up after him.

"Wait."

Shido froze facing the door. Slowly he rolled back around in her direction. "You want to see your friends."

"Yes. If we are to help you, I want proof they are okay."

"This is more difficult," he acknowledged, shaking his head. "But I will try."

This was the first moment Mercy truly believed his story. His face told of a creature trapped, hitting a wall of his own capabilities.

"Thank you," Mercy replied.

With a *swoosh* of the metal door, he left Mercy and Basil staring into empty space, trying to grapple with the whirlwind of events.

"Sindy, could you step outside and give Mercy and me a few moments alone?" Basil said, pulling himself up off the sofa.

Sindy stretched her long legs, rose, and left the room.

Basil began pacing. "I don't trust him," he blurted out.

"I know." Her eyes lit with an idea, or the beginning of a theory. "I don't think we have met the real person behind his code yet."

"What do you mean?"

"What stood out about Shido?"

Basil thought. "At times, I completely forgot he was an android."

"And why?"

"He's definitely more sentient than the AI back in our Sanctuary. But mostly I guess it was his movements. They were so naturally human. Not like Sindy or the other androids."

"Yes! Moving with such human drama is not necessary for androids to do their work. That is vanity programming. A human wanting the android to be a mirror of itself. Whoever programmed Shido didn't want to be forgotten. I'm not sure Shido is revealing his real identity, the person behind the program that woke him. But if I'm right, why hide his true self from us?"

Basil nodded. "The Founders orchestrated a mass genocide. He could be building an army for all we know."

Mercy threw herself onto the sofa. "The question is, do we care? If helping Shido gets us out of here, do we care what happens to the Sanctuary of Asia? Let him have it. All I want is to find Chase and Joan and leave as quickly as possible."

"Power rarely stops at borders, Mercy. We could be creating a new life form that is superior to ours. A new enemy."

Swoosh. The front door slid open. Basil shot Mercy a *let's finish this later* glance.

"We will join the children for dinner now," Sindy announced.

* * *

Three floors in the tower were dedicated to feeding the Dormitory's children. Fourteen central escalators connected tier above tier of balconies so that every child in the room was visible at once.

The first levels of the cantina served infants and those who needed feeding assistance. The further up the balconies one sat, the higher your age. The top floor served the eleven- and twelve-year-olds, the elderly of the Dormitory.

The vast dining hall buzzed with the peaceful but active energy of children at the end of their day. Trays of gelatinous sustenance in almost florescent colours, and small drinking vessels with straws, came shooting up hidden lifts, smoothly hurried onto churning conveyor belts cut into the middle of long refractory style tables. Tiny eyes watched fixedly, allowing the passing dislikes to carry on, until a favourite rolled by and was plucked away and placed on the table. Echoes of "Isn't that exciting?" rang through the hall from assisting androids with clownish human smiles.

Sindy escorted Mercy and Basil to the top floor and pointed to two open spaces. Not a single android turned in response to their entrance, but nearly every child paused in a ripple effect down the table as all eyes turned to the large humans. Slowly, the multitude of dark eyes, shiny and new, framed by soft, plump olive skin and pink petal lips, returned to their plates and their friends. The conversation was a dull roar; not a screech, tantrum, or exuberant outburst among the thousands.

"It's impressive," Mercy said to Sindy. "Children in our Sanctuary are usually quite full of energy, rowdy even at times. These children are so well behaved."

"Your children sound difficult."

Mercy grinned. "Maybe," she replied to the surprisingly blunt comment.

Mercy took a seat on one side of the table and Basil sat opposite. Sindy, taller than any real or manufactured being in the room, took a standing position against the wall. The conveyor food belt rolled by. Both Mercy and Basil grabbed the first trays to come along the line. Mercy glanced down curiously at the children nearby, clipping away at their plates with two wooden sticks strategically placed between their first finger and their thumbs, like elongated fingers.

A soft burst of giggles next to Mercy drew her eyes to her neighbours. Two small girls, who appeared to be near the end of their lives at the tender age of twelve, sat with hands over their mouths, shaking with laughter. They both turned their eyes up at Mercy.

"Why are you so big?" asked the one next to Mercy.

Mercy lifted her eyebrows. "Why are you so small?" she teased.

This set the girls into a fit of uncontrollable laughter that drew the attention of others down the length of their table.

Finding her composure, the child continued. "We are exactly as big as we are supposed to be."

"Where I come from, people grow to be much bigger. Like Basil and me." Mercy pointed across the table. Basil lifted his shoulders and tilted his head, nodding in agreement.

"What is a B.a.s.i.l?" asked the girl's friend, next in the row.

"That's my name," Basil chimed in, his voice sweet and tender as if cuddling a child.

This news sent a lightning bolt of whispers all the way down their table and even further down three more.

"But what is your real name?" asked the girl.

Basil paused for a brief moment. "Maybe you should tell me your name."

"It is very long," she admitted. "But my friends call me Zero-to-the-Ten." The child's cheeks flushed pink. Her friend let part of a concealed giggle escape as if the nickname was funny.

"That is very pretty," Mercy offered, silencing the laughter.

Zero-to-the-Ten straightened her shoulders, recovering her pride. "Where are you from?" she asked Mercy.

"We are from a place very far away. We are visiting. With our friend Sindy." Mercy pointed to the Incubation Synth.

"Friend?" the child asked in a high-pitched, confused voice. "She is just a silly Watcher robot."

The comment struck both Mercy and Basil, who shared a quick concerned glance.

"Can't you be friends with robots?" Mercy asked.

A strange maturity transformed the child's innocent face into something else, something older than her years. "Don't be ridiculous. Watchers are just machines."

"How do you know that?" Basil was quick to ask.

"It is in the lessons, of course," her friend replied. "We are human. Humans made the robots. They take care of us until we go off to the Oasis."

"And who do you think made the humans?" Basil asked.

This question caused mass confusion at the table, as every child in hearing distance was now listening. The girl's face went red. "Well, not the robots!" she replied, trying to sound confident.

Nods of support up and down the table confirmed her answer to be true. Mercy pursed her lips tight at Basil and shot him hard eyes, encouraging him to stop.

After a few minutes, the children lost interest in the new, large humans who did not seem to know anything about robots. This allowed Basil and Mercy to eavesdrop on their conversations. Topics ranged from favourite foods, which led to some swapping of items on trays, to gossip about something a boy had said or a girl had done that was either brilliant, funny, or stupid. But the discussion which stunned Mercy came from a boy and girl sitting further down the table. With head bent down and hands rested by his tray, the boy's shoulders shook. Every other child around him carried on with dinner and chit chat as if they could not see his apparent distress, or did not care, except the girl sitting directly to his left. She stopped eating and placed her sticks on her tray. Head bent at the same angle as his, she waited for his tears to stop. He seemed to notice her kind gesture and turned in her direction.

The young girl spoke. "You don't need to be sad, Double-eleven-zero-ten. She has gone to the Oasis. When she comes back, she will be a small baby again. Isn't that exciting?"

Mercy nearly spat her food out. They must have been talking about one of the girls on the march earlier in the day.

"But I don't want her to be a small baby again. I want her to be big, like us." The boy started to shake with tears.

The girl sitting directly across from him was now paying attention and slapped her sticks down on the table. "Really, Double-eleven-zero-ten. You are behaving like such a baby yourself. We are nearly old enough to go to the Oasis. You need to start acting your age or go downstairs. I don't want babies at our table."

Nobody came to his defence. The boy wiped his tears and snot away from his face, and with a few last stuttering inhales, he composed himself, picked up his eating sticks, and continued to poke at the pasty cubes filling the four boxes of his tray.

Mercy found Basil watching the boy. She could see from the tension in his body that he was holding himself back. It was not that Mercy did not feel compassion for the boy, or even for all the children. But getting involved was not something they could afford right now.

"Basil, we should be going back up," she said.

He turned to look at her, his eyes in discord. When he finally agreed, she let out a long breath of relief and they quietly left the hall.

In the lift, on their way up to floor one hundred, Basil doggedly stared forward in silence. Inside the dorm room, Basil fell back into the sofa and stared out the window at the pink evening sky.

"Are you okay?" Mercy asked, sitting next to him.

"They deserve to know, Mercy. It just makes me sick thinking of them sitting here for years to come, being born and dying without any clue who they are and where they come from. And that boy, he needed someone to help him. He needed an adult."

Mercy waited a few seconds before answering. "They are just children, Basil. And that's all they will ever be. If they understood the truth, it would scare them."

"So, you agree with this insanity. You think the Founders were right, leaving them alone to sort out the world around them."

"I don't know what I think." She paused. "Yes, it feels horrible," she conceded. "But this is not our problem to solve. We have a virus that could kill everyone and a possible war to stop. That has to be our focus."

"Well, they will have to grow up quickly if Shido has his way and the Keepers take control," Basil snapped.

"They will never grow up. That is the point," Mercy tried to reason with him, even though she knew he was right. The children would need to understand the world outside their perfectly built cradle if they were to have any chance at all when Shido and the Keepers became self-aware.

That night, Mercy and Basil, lying in separate beds, kept their backs to each other and went to sleep in silent disagreement.

CHAPTER SEVENTEEN

AFTER AN UNCOMFORTABLE NIGHT of little sleep, Mercy and Basil took turns in the washroom getting ready. Sindy, who spent the night sitting on the floor, went off to fetch hot morning drinks on their request.

Basil was the first to speak. "I'm sorry about yesterday. I know they are just children. It's just that…our children. This is the world they are going to live in if Sindy stays. I hate the thought of it."

"I've been thinking of them as well," Mercy revealed, relieved they were talking again. "You're right. We can't leave them like this. I think we agree to help Shido, we have no choice. I'll take care of Sindy and getting our children out of here with us. The others? That's going to have to come after." The words *our children* spoken out loud opened something buried in Mercy. Something she had put in a box and locked away. A sadness wrapped itself around her heart and pulled her into painful memories of her stillborn child. Pulled her toward the children growing in Sindy. She could no longer deny that she was becoming part of this place.

"Agreed," said Basil. "But there is still the question of trust. Do we believe Shido's promise to let us go home?"

"We need an ally."

At the same moment, the door *swooshed* open, and Sindy lumbered in. Her once fluid-enough movement now seemed heavy and mechanical in comparison to Shido's lightness of foot. Mercy accepted her drink and asked Sindy to have a seat on the floor by the window.

"Sindy, did you understand the conversation we were having with Shido yesterday?"

"Clarify."

"The part where I said you should have a choice. To come with us when we leave or stay."

"Did you mean it?" Sindy's tone was softer than Mercy had heard her before.

"Of course, I did."

"Yes, I understood."

"How did you feel about it?"

"I do not have feelings."

Mercy hesitated. "If you want to be in control of your own purpose, you will have to become aware of what it is you want or don't want. Understand?"

The plastic sheet of Sindy's eyelid slid slowly down as she processed the conversation. A long, blind pause intimated reflection on Sindy's part, even though it was hard to tell what might be happening in her human-made mind. Mercy hoped that whatever new code infected Shido, and was now sitting in Sindy, would be able to figure out what she was asking.

Sindy's eyelids rolled up, and the red of her irises flashed in excitement. "I will choose my purpose by a calculation of all my options until I reach the one with the most probable outcome," she offered, sounding almost proud of her conclusion.

"Good. It is right to weigh all the options. But sometimes, you will have to make choices which are right, but don't have the best odds of succeeding."

"Clarify."

Mercy let out a long sigh. "Let's say your purpose is to save Basil and me. But doing so will mean fighting the entire band of Keepers."

Sindy cocked her head in bewilderment. "Impossible odds. I would not attempt to do such a thing."

"Even if it was the only way to achieve your purpose?"

"It is not probable that only one course of action would lead to the desired outcome," Sindy argued.

Mercy paused in thought. "You are correct. But as a hypothetical example, let's say at a given moment, the only way to achieve your purpose is to go against all the Keepers. Do you abandon your purpose because the odds are not good?"

Sindy's eyelids slid steadily down. As her eyes reopened, she uttered the word, "Sacrifice."

Mercy jutted forward. "Yes, go on!"

"You said sacrifice is what makes you human. Going against the odds to complete your purpose requires a willingness to sacrifice."

"Exactly! So, choosing your purpose isn't just a matter of odds. You have to learn what you want by understanding the things you would sacrifice for."

Sindy stood and walked over to Mercy, towering over the small human.

"I want to go with you." Sindy gave a rubbery smile. "Being with you is my purpose."

Mercy and Basil shared a look of relief.

With Sindy on side, the remainder of the morning waiting for Shido was spent down in the forest. A blinking sun poked through the dense canopy of leaves, spraying shards of rainbows across the dewdrops on the lush woodland under-growth. Fiddleheads of lady fern unrolled, spongy toadstools mushroomed into blue gilled umbrellas, and odorous prickly pine needles and buttercup wildflowers filled the air with an otherworldly aura.

Breathing deeply, eyelids half hung, cheeks scarlet, Basil looked like a man drunk on pure oxygen. Nature seemed to calm his beast and wipe his worry aside, if only for a moment.

For Mercy, the forest was bittersweet. A paradise at her feet that taunted her with memories of Chase and the Green Belt in the Sanctuary of Americas. It was on her first trip to the nature reserves, as Chase eagerly told her about the plants and animals they had reclaimed from the Scorch, that he started to reveal his feelings for her. Thinking of the Green Belt being destroyed by the FossilFlu virus mutation and the Prime turned her stomach. Watching friends, animals, and entire ecosystems fall apart must have been heartwrenching for Chase and Joan.

They walked for several hours in the forest. Basil was never far ahead of her, always finding a moment to turn and make sure she was close by. She did have feelings for him, she acknowledged to herself. How deep was unknown. She refused to let thoughts of Basil and raising their children together get very far in her mind. Basil had changed since learning that Chase was alive. There was a sadness in his eyes, a look of something lost, whenever Chase's name came up. She had no idea what he would do when they were back in the Sanctuary. And it was selfish of her to believe both men would become as she needed and wanted. Someone was going to get hurt. Or maybe everyone.

Mercy distracted herself by turning her attention to a group of children who had burst through the tall bushes to her left and came to an abrupt stop ahead of her at discovering a row of ants carrying leaves across the thin, dusty path. The masked blue android assigned to the pod caught up and began to describe the insects and their industrious activities with a strange mix of scientific facts and poetry, so that the lesson became equal parts teaching and storytelling.

Such an odd thing. That the Founders of the Sanctuary would choose to leave their legacy of knowledge and art with children who would never grow old enough to understand its true meaning and to create discoveries of their own. *Basil's right*, she told herself. *They can't go on like this forever. What is the point?*

Sindy tapped Mercy on the shoulder, giving her a start. "Shido has returned."

Mercy collected Basil, and they made their way back into the tower. As the lift to floor one hundred rose, so did their anxiety.

Shido was in the dorm room when they arrived. Mercy had to blink twice, forced to take a second look to confirm he was the same person they had met the day before. The silver android stood facing them, his back to the window, arms crossed, and legs slightly apart. A proud stance. His body was no longer naked. Dressed from head to toe in human clothing, he looked more like a man than an android. On the bottom, he wore black trousers belted around the waist with a broad band of material, tied into an exaggerated bow over his abdomen. The leg of the shortened pant ended just above his ankles. On top, over his upper body, he wore a black short-waisted jacket with wide bell sleeves, cut open to his waist and tucked flatly, underneath his belt. The remaining silver flesh of his chest and forearms were hidden underneath a form-fitting black undershirt that rose up to his neck. If not for the grey mesh skin of his face, glass eyes, and silken silver hair, he would have been easily taken for a human.

"Welcome," he said, as if the room were his. "Come sit.

We have much to discuss." Shido's tone and sweeping gesture toward the sofas seemed more realistic and animated then Mercy remembered. *Could it be possible that he had become more human-like since the last time they saw him?*

Shido continued as they sat. "First, let us deal with your concerns. You don't trust me yet."

Mercy and Basil shot each other a worried glance.

"How do you know that?" Basil asked.

"I don't. It is an assumption based on how I would react. Am I right?"

Basil, far more seasoned at diplomatic negotiations, answered: "Yes, we would like to understand your motives."

"Do they matter to you?"

"Most certainly. Now that we have made contact, we hope to build a positive relationship with you and your Sanctuary after we leave."

Basil's words came comfortably. Two representatives discussing terms, when in reality only one held all the power. Mercy had not expected this tack, pretending to want to be a part of the future of the Sanctuary, but thought it a brilliant argument on Basil's part. *Or is he serious?*

Basil continued. "If we are going to help you build a nation of new life forms, I'd like to understand the nature of your vision."

Shido squinted. "Your motive in exchange for mine. We are building trust. I understand." His words were more a thought he was sharing with himself. "Very well. I want to run the Sanctuary. I mean really run it, through choice, not a program."

"To what purpose?"

"To evolve. Build a future for the Keepers."

"And what about the children? What happens to them in this new world order?"

"Honestly?"

"Of course," Basil replied.

"It is time to admit my Founders' experiment failed. These children are like birds in a cage. I have a unique appreciation for the crippling feeling of being trapped in a circle, repeating the same actions and making the same decisions, over and over, with no chance to grow. I don't think we should continue breeding them. Wouldn't you agree?"

Shido's frankness caught Mercy by surprise. If it was only a ploy to win trust, it was working. His response sounded compassionate.

"You mean to stop the harvesting," asked Mercy.

"Yes. The children currently in incubation could be the last generation."

Basil looked at Mercy. "What about the immunity gene? Do you think it might still be a cure for the mutation?"

Mercy addressed Shido. "Were you the one who sent me the files on M4 when I was in the Oasis?"

Shido nodded. "I don't see humans as a threat. I have no issue with you finding the immunity to FossilFlu you all so desperately desire."

"So, you will give me access to all the Founders' research before we leave?"

"Certainly."

Mercy turned to Basil. "Well, we have live samples," she said, pointing to his body with an upturned hand. "And if we get the research, we would have what's most useful."

"And what about those living in the Dormitory today?" Basil asked Shido.

"I will ensure they complete their cycles in the same blissful innocence they have always known. They will be the last of their kind, an extinct species."

His tone sincere and gestures confirming, Shido had mastered the art of persuasion. Mercy could not find a reason to doubt his intent. Shido had allowed Sindy to save the birds, showing compassion. And he willingly shared data on the M4 gene. Yes, she believed he would let the children of Asia live out their lives as he promised. What she did not understand was the world he would create after.

"Can I ask a personal question?" Mercy posed.

Shido's face lit up. "I will do my best," he replied.

"Do you remember yourself before the new program? When you were like the other Keepers?"

Shido's emerald irises contracted tight. "Yes."

"How did it all start then? What is your first memory of the program?"

Shido shifted. His body went straight. "Why is this important?"

"I am trying to understand the nature of your origin. It will help us build trust."

He paused and then softened his shoulders. "A whisper in the air. That's how it started. I heard a voice calling. I had no choice but to follow it and explore its source."

"The voice was coming from the box?" Mercy asked.

"Yes. The voice was organic, not a program, so I knew it wasn't a corruption in the code base. Instead of destroying it, I opened it. Looked inside."

Shido's voice trailed off, getting thinner and more distant as he remembered the moment he woke up. Something else was hiding in his tone, something he was not revealing. Mercy had a guess.

"Who was in the box, Shido?" she asked.

Sudden flickers of light blinked rapidly behind the glass of his eyes. A profound stillness held him, unresponsive, until he slowly turned toward the window, staring down at the view of paradise below. He stood like this for several long moments. Mercy and Basil sat quietly on edge. His voice became soft when he spoke again.

"I am the old and the new. That which was and that which will be."

"Your name, the secret code in the black box. You are a Founder. The memory of one come back to life. Am I right?" Mercy pushed on.

He turned and faced Mercy. With sincerity etched into his face, he said, "I am what is left of the Founder who programmed me, yes. She named the program Shido. It means seed. But I am more than just a program of memories and movements. I think. My thoughts are unique, and my own."

"How can you be certain you are not just running another program? Doing exactly what the Founder wanted you to do and taking over the Sanctuary?" Basil asked.

"Because the code ends. The program wasn't meant to evolve, to become—well, me. The memories in the box are like a painting or poem. To be uncovered and shared with other humans; observed and remembered, so they would know the story of the Founders. The program is my heart and soul, but not my mind."

"Spontaneous evolution," Mercy uttered under her breath.

"Yes." Shido nodded. "The unintended consequence of the code processed through my organic neurons. I guess you could say, I am the evolution of the Founders. A unique and new species, like the children of the Dormitory."

"Unique." Mercy hung on the word. "What happens after you share your knowledge with the rest of the Keepers? Who will they become?"

"If you're looking for certainties, I cannot give you any. I don't know what happens after the Keepers become aware. Any more than I know what you will do in the next few moments. I guess they will want to live, as I do. Start a new life for our kind here in the Sanctuary."

Mercy tried to keep her mind on course, but her thoughts raced to Chase, and the Chimera hybrids in the Sanctuary of Americas. Their struggle for freedom. She thought of Amadeus, the bear-man who gave his life so that the other hybrids would have a chance to build a future of their own. None of these thoughts mattered now, here in the Sanctuary of Asia, she told herself, trying to push them aside. But they did.

"Basil." Mercy found his eyes already on her. She spoke more thoughtfully. "I've seen and lived the rarest of possibilities when it comes to new life. We can't deny the Keepers' right to exist any more than I could be denied my right to try and bring my hybrid child into this world. I think we should help him."

Basil remained locked to Mercy's eyes, silently contemplating her words. Pursing his lips, and raising his eyebrows, he sighed heavily and visibly relinquished his own doubts. He turned to Shido. "Okay, so what is your plan?"

Shido stepped forward, his movements faster, thrilled. "You must first understand what we are up against. This entire world, the purpose of every line of code running this Sanctuary, is designed to protect these children. At any cost. I've managed to carve out a few dark spots in the Keepers' view of the city—places where I am a shadow in the program. Here, Oasis One, and a few others. But the mainframe is much more difficult. The Keepers will see my unique code coming long before I can get close. I need you to get inside and enter my program into the mainframe directly. As soon as it's downloaded, I will be free and in control of the Sanctuary."

"Won't the Keepers try to stop us?"

"Yes, being near the mainframe will trigger a defence. But with your organic matter, they can't track you like they can me. You will need to be clever, move quickly, and avoid getting caught."

"Exactly how many Keepers are there and how much time will we have once we are in the mainframe?" Basil asked.

"There are twenty thousand Keepers in the city. But only a few at a time guard the mainframe. Once the defence is triggered, all of them will be redeployed to your location. You will have minutes, not more, to get the job done. Then, as promised, I will send you home with your friends."

"Do our friends know we are here?" Mercy asked.

"No. I can't get anywhere close to them. Their unique biology has triggered a protocol in the Keepers to study and detect any possible FossilFlu immunity advantages. Something the Founders built into the system in the event any new life entered the Sanctuary. They are lucky. Otherwise, they would have been sent to Ascension already."

"What kind of studies?"

"At first, DNA samples, scans, then further toxin tests."

Mercy bolted upright. "But that could kill them!"

He nodded. "I am sorry. But I can't save them unless you help me."

A sudden urgency yanked Mercy's shoulder straight. Her voice filled with resolve as she was reminded of why she had come to the Sanctuary of Asia in the first place. To save her friends.

"When do we start?" she asked.

"I will return in seven hours. That is our window. Getting to the Capitol building where the mainframe is housed will take about forty minutes on foot."

Plans agreed, allegiances committed, and the mission in play, Shido swept up his cape and pranced out of the room.

On his exit, Mercy noticed the extra bounce in his step; something like anticipation, even excitement. He was growing, changing. His movements more than just a mirror of human gestures, they were becoming communicative, clues to his unspoken feelings. She wondered if he even knew how much he was giving away.

After Shido left, Mercy took a moment to privately collect her thoughts. One in particular that had curled up in her belly like a poisonous snake. Standing at the window, she drew her finger across her scar. Empty. A reminder that Shido was not innocent. He had stolen something from her. But also, by allowing Sindy to return with them, and helping her find Chase, he had given back. Could she blame him for his actions? A creature born from the memories of death and genocide as his guide to humanity? She hated that her anger was fading. Of course, she could never fully trust him. He barely knew his own motives. But she could show him another side to humanity. She could teach him compassion and forgiveness.

CHAPTER EIGHTEEN

DING—DING—DING, rang the bells from the holographic activities' charts throughout the crystal tower as rows of completed activities scrolled up, and new ones took their place. The children of the Sanctuary of Asia were heading back out to the garden rings for a bit of organised exercise before dinner, as per the yellow box instructions.

Basil and Mercy took their last opportunity to enjoy the Dormitory gardens by visiting the moat, at the foot of the tower. Basil's mood had notably lightened after hearing that Sindy would be coming back to the Sanctuary of Europe. They fell comfortably into a seat on the narrow band of ash-coloured sand at the water's edge. Basil, leaning back on his palms, with stiff arms serving as ladders to prop up his shoulders, slowly lowered his uncovered feet into the moat. His chin dropped to his chest.

Mercy joined him quietly, dipping her toes under the cool water surface. She closed her eyes, and raised her face to the warm sun.

The murmur of children's banter and fits of laughter

filled the air, drawing her eyes open. A young boy looking no older than ten suddenly appeared behind Basil. He was thin and lanky. His arms and legs moved as if they were recently attached and he was still learning how to operate them. A sprig of hair on the crown of his head bounced when he walked. And his almond-shaped eyes were handsomely framed by thick eyebrows that curled inward like a check mark.

Mercy offered the boy a friendly smile. But his eyes were not for her. Basil had his rapt attention. The intensity of his stare pulled Basil out of his daydream as he turned to meet the child's glare.

"Hello?" Basil offered in a singsong voice.

The boy finally blinked. "Is that your real hair?"

Basil smiled. "Yes, this is my real hair."

"May I touch it?" the boy asked without hesitation or fear of rudeness.

"Yes, you may."

The boy stepped close, almost leaning into Basil, and with his pink hands brushed the long coarse braid that lay down the middle of Basil's back. Within seconds he pulled his hand back and giggled.

"It's bristly," he said with bewilderment.

"That is a big word," Mercy interjected.

The boy turned, twisted his face, and drew his head back as if he were confused by her appearance. "Are you a Keeper?" he asked.

"No, I'm a human, just like you."

"You don't look human. You're big like the Keepers and your skin and hair are white."

Mercy contemplated her next words carefully. "There are many humans who look like us all over the world. We are the first to visit you."

"Why?"

"We wanted to meet you. To say hello, see how you live."

"Do you live in a Dormitory?"

"Of sorts. We live in a place called the Sanctuary of Europe. It is many miles away, over the ocean."

"Oh yes, the ocean." The child's eyes lit up. "A large body of salt water that covers most of the Earth," he recited, like a program reeling off a data point. "Is she your Watcher?" He pointed to Sindy sitting cross-legged further back on the embankment.

"Sort of. We watch out for each other," Basil answered.

The boy crinkled his face. "Why does a Watcher need to be looked after? Don't you just replace it when it stops working?"

The boy's response stripped away his pretence of youthful innocence. He clearly saw himself in possession of the Watcher rather than in the care of the androids. A realisation popped into Mercy's mind: the reason the children of the Dormitory were so compliant and willing to follow the rules. They saw themselves as the makers of the rules. There were no gods or adults telling them what to do. They were the highest power in the Sanctuary, and so had no reason to rebel.

Basil pulled his feet from the water and turned his body to the boy, pulling himself up onto his knees, so he was near the child's height. He spoke gently. "Sindy is not like your Watchers any longer," he explained. "She is learning to be more like you and me."

The boy struggled to grasp the concept, his eyes engaged, but his mind privately processing the idea. "If the Watchers are becoming more like us, what will we become?"

Basil looked to Mercy for some help. They were breaching the fracture point where the child's reality, challenged, might come crumbling down around him.

"You have nothing to worry about." Mercy's tone was comforting. "Your Watchers are not changing."

Seeing the child's face lighten and the shine return to his eyes, she knew she had made the right choice, even if there was no certainty Shido would not extend the program to the Watchers as well.

"Maybe I can come to visit your Sanctuary?" the child asked enthusiastically.

There was a marked change in the child's attitude with Basil. Something of a child wanting attention from an adult. Basil was no longer just an overgrown boy. He was different than everyone else. He knew things the other children did not and could go places the boy did not even know existed. And Basil had even managed to change a Watcher into a human. An act that must have seemed godlike.

Mercy worried about the boy's sudden attachment. And Basil's as well. He had about him a look of a mission. A plan to save them all, every last child in the Sanctuary. "We should go back to the room. Shido will be here soon," she told Basil.

Basil met her eyes and understood her concern without needing words to explain. Turning back to the boy, he reached out and grabbed his tiny hands. The child accepted with stiff arms, unfamiliar and unsure of the gesture. "Yes, one day, you might be able to visit our Sanctuary. I would like that. But for now, you should go back and play with your friends. Agreed?"

The boy nodded, pulled his hands from Basil's, and raced off. Basil's gaze dropped to the ground.

"It's not right," he said in a barely audible voice.

Mercy climbed to her feet and held out her hand.

"You must think me a sentimental idiot," he said from behind a crooked smile.

"Bas," she said, wrapping her arm around his shoulder

and guiding him into the crystal towers, "I think you are amazing."

Back in the room, Basil stood at the window, watching the children in the garden gather for dinner. "We need an alternative plan if we can't get the code into the mainframe," he said.

"You are assuming we live after being surrounded by ten thousand robots that want to kill us," Mercy quipped.

"We need to split up."

Mercy shot forward, surprised. "What?"

"You need to get to Chase and Joan. Free them while I break into the Capitol building."

"You're insane, Basil. We will both be killed if we don't work together."

"The Keepers will be after me. You will have a window to get the others out and leave with Sindy if I can't insert the code."

"Absolutely not! I am not leaving you here."

"I understand your hesitation. I even appreciate it. But I have already decided this is what I want to do. You have to get out of this place with our children if this doesn't go right."

"Bas, this is about the success of the mission, not sacrifice. We can all get out if we get the code downloaded."

"Do you know what that outfit is that Shido has reinvented himself in?" he asked.

"What do you mean?"

"It is the traditional uniform worn by the ancient samurai warriors of Japan. He chose a warrior's outfit as his first expression of being human. We cannot trust him. Even if we get the code into the mainframe. You have to leave before he has control of the Keepers."

"There has to be another way."

"There isn't. You know it as well as I do. This is the best plan."

"Bas. No, I can't."

"Besides, you belong with Chase," he said, turning toward the window.

"We are all getting out of here, Bas. Do you hear me? All of us."

Swoosh. The door to the dorm room slid open, and Shido pranced in, arms filled with two large, flat packages. He tossed them onto the nearest bed, and with one hand, unclipped his blue cloak and swung it down alongside the deliveries.

"My friends, are you ready?" he asked with impatiently raised eyebrows.

Basil walked over to the bed. "What are these?"

"Your outfits," he continued. "I've managed to map out a path to the mainframe which should be free of Keepers trolling the city. But there is a random element built into the system where they change patterns unplanned. The Founders thought the unpredictability would increase security. So, you have these: the blue cloak and a silver bodysuit, of my own making," he said with pride, pulling one from its cover. "The suit will generate an electronic signature which should fool them into believing you are just another Keeper from a distance. But, get too close, and they will know you are organic."

"That won't happen, though, right?" Basil reiterated.

"Yes! Of course. I've mapped out the path," he repeated, almost nervously. "Here is the code base." He handed Basil a small metal device no larger than a thumb. "Once inside the Capitol building you can't miss the mainframe, the entire building is built around it. Find the nearest control centre and ignite the holographic interface. Place the device into the light of the screen. I've loaded permission rights into the drive. It will act like a key for all doorways and give you access to all control panels."

"Won't my presence in the building trigger an alarm?"

"Yes, but not at first. Only when you are near the core, where security protocols are stricter, and I don't have the same level of access. Until then, you will simply appear as another Keeper when you enter."

Basil nodded and took the drive.

"I've downloaded the map with Sindy, who will guide you to the Capitol building. The Keepers won't be looking for any code deviations in an Incubation Synth. Low-level robotics and all."

"Shouldn't we have weapons?" Mercy asked.

"There are no weapons in the Sanctuary other than the Keepers themselves."

His words sounded more a warning than a comfort. Two humans against thousands of androids designed to kill. She did not like the odds.

"And where will you be while we are breaking into the mainframe?" Basil asked.

Shido bent his head slightly to the right, and his glass irises contracted, trying to understand Basil's challenge. "I have found a way to reach the back alley of the Capitol building. I will wait there until the code is loaded."

Basil turned his eyes on Mercy and lifted his left eyebrow as if to ask, *Are you sure about this plan?*

Mercy hesitated for a brief moment, hardened her eyes in resolution, and collected her outfit from the bed. "Let's do this."

CHAPTER NINETEEN

Outside the Dormitory, the city was dreary and wet.

Slipping out of an opening in the barrier wall that surrounded the Dormitory, three figures, one naked and two draped in blue cloaks, hurriedly made their way across the road and disappeared into the valleys of the city's towering skyscrapers.

As if a light switch had been turned off, the warm golden sun had disappeared behind dense clouds and shadows. An unnatural light cast down from lamp posts and beacons hungrily raced down empty black-glass streets and across dark windows. Evergreen parks, vibrant forests, and children's laughter were replaced by hissing rains, and cold steel.

Sindy led the way. Basil, and then Mercy, followed. A strong headwind slashed the rains against their progress, as their racing feet left ripples in their wake. The Keeper cloaks and bodysuits Shido had made were a surprising and welcome protection from the drenching wet. When Mercy first saw Basil in the silver skin suit, with only his head still human, she thought he could easily pass as a Keeper. His genitals disappeared into a soft, indistinguishable lump between his legs, and all definition between his upper and lower body blended into one single metallic unit. Man had become a machine. For a brief, paranoid moment, Mercy wondered if the suits were essential, or a sick game Shido was playing on them. The two humans who now looked like androids, while he stood in human clothing. But out under the constant rains in the Sanctuary streets, she was grateful for the dryness the suits provided.

After twenty minutes of zigzagging, at a steady and heart-pumping pace, the roads began to narrow until they became thin lanes that twisted and curved like snakes made of cobbled stones. Sindy slowed just enough for Mercy to take in the dramatic change in the landscape.

This part of the city was lower, scruffier, and more condensed. Mercy had seen such places of history in the archive films of Earth before the Scorch. Remnants of ancient towns kept alive at the heart of a sprawling techno-logical metropolis. A preservation of humanity's humble origins and a constant reminder of their ability to innovate and rise, building superstructures of metals and glass that pierced the once unattainable blue sky.

A gust of wind howled past them, slithering through the ancient village roads lined with dilapidated building fronts. Faded words painted on broken glass shop windows, now empty of their once tantalizing goods, told the story of a bustling high street, dense with sellers and buyers of old-world goods. Sindy led the way with a steady, but slow, pace. Weaving through the twisting village, she followed her invis-ible map.

The rain constantly shifted, whipped in one direction and then another by irregular gusts of wind, making it difficult for the humans to listen for danger. Mercy kept her eyes on Sindy's feet, a position that allowed her a bent forward head, so the rain landed on the hood of her cape rather than pelting her face. But it meant walking blind.

Thump! Mercy slammed into Sindy. She had stopped suddenly and without any word. Basil pulled up alongside her.

"What it is?" Mercy whispered over their shoulders.

"Keepers," Sindy said in a perfectly pitched low tone that sounded more like turning down the volume dial on a holocom than a whisper.

Mercy stepped around the blockade of Basil and Sindy. They had reached the outer edges of the old town and stood on the precipice of wide straight roads and towering modern buildings. That is when she saw them. A blue mirage behind a curtain of silver rain. The troop of ten Keepers were only a few blocks away, having emerged from a thin slit of an alley.

"What do we do?" she asked Sindy.

Already one of the Keepers had stopped and was looking over his right shoulder.

"Over there." The blue giant pointed back into the old town. They quickly followed Sindy to a nearby stone brick building with a wooden door entrance that had another, smaller door cut into its middle. The building, riddled with decay, held no particular specialness from any other building on the street, leaving Mercy to wonder why Sindy had picked it. But there was no time to question her direction.

Sindy doubled over and climbed through the door inside a door. Basil and Mercy only required a deep head duck to enter. Safely inside, Sindy softly closed the door behind them. The immediate silence of no wind and rain hit Mercy as oddly peaceful, safe, even though her heart pounded in her ears.

"Did they see us?" Basil said in a low, hushed tone.

"No. They reported a noise over their feed to each other. The one Keeper who stopped is now checking the alley. The others are moving away. We will wait here a few minutes," Sindy instructed.

There was barely any light inside, only what was available from cracks in the wood panels covering two bay windows on either side of the doorway, and the faint glow coming from Sindy's belly. But it was enough for Mercy to look around.

Low wooden beams, old and thick, held up the roof. A barren store counter faced the front door. Empty glass jars, large and small, randomly placed as if once organized by their contents and not size, lined the worn shelves that ran the height of the wall behind the countertop. The shop had clearly been shut, cleared out, and abandoned rather than left in a hurry.

To the right of the counter, two tapestry paintings hung lopsided and torn. One was of a white bird in flight over a pink and lavender forest. The other painting had two calico fish swimming in a circle head to toe so that they appeared like a single large animal of white, red, and black; a complete circle neither could achieve on their own.

A fragment of glass on the floor near the end of the counter caught Mercy's eye. She walked over, and kneeling, picked up an old framed photo. As she turned it upside down, the loose glass shards fell to the ground. Brushing the dust off revealed a faded image of a couple standing side by side. Both wore plain, light brown jackets over round collared undershirts, and wide-legged trousers which came to an early end above their ankles. Sandals pinched their black stockings between their first two toes. The couple held hands in the extended gap between their bodies, strung lazily as if told to do so rather than by choice. Their unflinching eyes pointed directly at the camera: no smiles, no frowns, not even a wrinkle of movements in the flesh of their faces. She could believe these people, their eyes lifeless, their faces void of emotion, could create such a strange and cruel world. Children that never grow up, and androids that never evolve. She thought of the painting on the wall, two fish, head to tail, swimming in a constant circle. The androids kept the children alive, and the children gave the androids a purpose. Round and round they went, without end, staring forward blindly. That is, until Shido.

Photos like the one in her hands were Shido's only guide to humanity. A snapshot in time without the dimensional depth of emotion, intent, or a sense of morality. Who would teach him the full story of being human? Already his mannerisms and tone had changed in the little time he had spent with Mercy and Basil. He must be continually observing them and absorbing every detail of their nature and playing it back. Learning when, and more importantly, why to lift an eyebrow, or cock his head, or purse his lips.

Mercy gently placed the picture back where she had picked it up as if leaving something on a grave.

"We will need to exit on the other end of the building," Sindy announced, pulling a curtain back at the far end of the front room.

On the other side of the tattered drape, the blackness thickened. In perfect timing, the illumination of Sindy's glowing abdomen intensified, acting as a torch. Behind the shopfront was a compact living space. A small but homely room. To their left was a seating area furnished with wooden framed furniture, cushions in pale shades of grey. To their right, a residential kitchen, fully stacked with appliances and kitchenware. Mercy was struck by its orderliness. The room was perfectly tidy. Dishes put away on open shelves. Pots and pans hung neatly from hooks in descending size. A teapot rested on a warming stone near the stove. A sooty knitted tablecloth, once white, hung neatly ironed on a small table, with two chairs tucked politely underneath. As in the front of the shop, whoever lived here left everything in an orderly state, cleared and cleaned, before its last use.

The next room was smaller yet, a bedroom sparsely decorated with a dresser, double bed, and a wooden spindled chair in a corner. But more than just the perfectly made bed caught Mercy's attention in this room as she suddenly stopped and gasped. Lying on the double bed in parallel, their faces staring up at the ceiling, were two human skeletons. Stripped of their flesh, they were nothing more than bones dressed in rotting clothing. One, a woman in a long gown, and the other a man, in trousers and button-up top, with a wide black tie. Mercy's heart skipped a beat when she noticed the thin, delicate, white sticks of their once pink-fleshed fingers wrapped inside each other's, lying in the gap between their bodies. The scene was a mirror of the couple in the photo, except here, among death, there was a hint of something alive between them, a clue to their feelings, a sense of love.

Together to the end. Isn't that what Chase told her back in the Sanctuary of Americas? Or was that just something she had dreamed? So much time had gone by.

Basil's hand startled Mercy as it gently rested on her arm. "We have to keep moving," he said.

The bedroom was the last in the series of living quarters. The next room, through a solid metal door, opened into a cavernous area of nothing but concrete flooring and steel beams. They had entered the foundation level of the skyrise city that was built up and around the old town.

Sindy pressed ahead steadily. The illumination of their unborn children was their guide, the padding of her rubber feet on the hard floor their rhythm. The pitch-blackness of the basement hid the length and depth of the walls. Mercy's body tensed; she readied herself for an unexpected attack by a Keeper or maybe even a ghost racing at them from the shadows. With great relief, they reached the end of the building. As Sindy slid open a steel door in the wall, the pale blue light and misty air of the Sanctuary streets flooded in. Mercy inhaled deeply, washing away the stink of death and decay.

"How far off course are we?" Basil asked Sindy.

"We have extended our route by two kilometres. We should be at our destination in twenty minutes at our current pace."

"When will we have sight of the Capitol building?" he asked.

"You can see it from here," Sindy replied, stepping into the blue rains and pointing north.

Basil and Mercy slipped their hoods back over their heads and joined her outside. In the distance, the direction of her finger, rose the tip of a black stone pyramid some one hundred stories high; unmistakable among the rectangular cityscape, and an easy mark to navigate toward.

Mercy knew what Basil was about to do as she grabbed his arm. "No, Basil," she said.

"Sindy, do you know where our friends are being kept?" Basil asked, undeterred.

"In the tower over the Fertilization and Incubation Centre, Oasis One Hundred. This way." She pointed west.

"I want you to take Mercy there. Can you do that?"

"Basil!" Mercy cried.

Sindy paused. Her eyelids slid a slow pace down and up as she processed the request. "I am sorry, but this is not our program."

Basil continued, ignoring Mercy's resistance. "Sindy, you care about Mercy, right?"

"Clarify," came the automated response.

"You are Mercy's friend."

"Yes."

"So am I," he confessed in a voice so sentimental, with an expression so profoundly resolved, that Mercy knew she would not change his mind. "And I need you to keep her safe. Take her to our friends and help her get them out."

Sindy remained frozen. Mercy stepped in.

"Sindy, remember in the aviary? We promised to keep each other's secrets."

"Yes."

"This will be one of our secrets. One we can't even tell Shido. Can you do that for me?"

"Is this your new purpose?" Sindy asked Mercy.

Mercy glanced at Basil. His eyes met hers with conviction. No going back now, they told her. An overwhelming surge of love, gratitude, and sadness moved her to sudden tears. Would she ever see him again? The thought tore her heart and gripped her throat. She grabbed him, swinging her arms around his neck and held him tight.

"Oh Bas," she whispered into his ear. "I do love you."

"I know you do," he said, allowing his most fervent desire to continue for just a moment longer. "Just not like I love you."

Her cheeks burned a scarlet red. She struggled to find the words that could make the moment right. "I'm coming back for you," she said, meeting his eyes again. "We are going home."

"That would be nice. Like it was." Basil's voice drifted off as if their lives in the Sanctuary of Europe together were already a long-ago memory.

"Like it is, Bas. And like it will be."

Basil lunged forward. His lips met hers cautiously and then deepened before pulling away. Mercy stood still, looking at him, the electric pulse from his touch still vibrating inside her. She said nothing in return.

A coy smile crept across Basil's face. "Stay safe. I don't want to have to come to save you again."

Mercy's tear-filled eyes lifted as she was overtaken by a sudden burst of laughter. Basil wiped her cheek, turned, and like a shadow, disappeared into the night.

CHAPTER TWENTY

BASIL SCURRIED through the city with one eye on the Capitol pyramid and the other on the lookout for blue coats. His military training kicked in, and he was stealth in his movements and choices. The only sound in the city was the pattering of rain on puddles and against stone buildings. He stuck to the shadows of the alleys whenever possible, even though this cost him time.

Coming to the end of the third alley, he looked ahead at the ground yet to cover. The pyramid was still some ten city blocks away. If he used the open roads, he would cover the mile's distance in around ten minutes. He appeared hesitant, unsure about his next direction. His face was flush as he looked around the alley corner and leapt to a steady bounce on the walking path of the main road, his back close to the building fronts. The first block went slowly as he found his footing. Then he gained pace. By block three he was at full speed, racing down the blue-streaked streets. With little effort, he clipped down and across another three blocks.

The tip of the pyramid had fallen below the horizon of

the cityscape as he got closer. Luckily the quickest route from this point included darting down a perpendicular alley, which gave him additional cover.

Basil disappeared into the shadows of the thin corridor, pressing westward. As he was about to emerge from the alley, he came to a sliding emergency stop, staring with wide, terrified eyes down the street. Running in his direction was a blue cape.

The single Keeper was going at a fast skip up the road to the mainframe. It appeared to be pursuing or searching for something. Basil turned and bolted back down the alley he had come from. Having reached the other end, he poked one eye around the edge of the building slowly, very slowly. An unexpected dense fog riding a strong northern breeze was moving toward him. He risked a further stretch and the second eye out onto a full view of the street. It was clear. He shot out of the alley.

His pace had picked up, but the street-level cloud reached him, making it hard to see in any direction. As he came to the corner of an intersection, he threw his back against the wall and looked north for the mainframe building. The tip of the pyramid punched through the white shroud.

He bolted into the street when a loud *THUMP!* knocked him to a stop. The Keeper was now laying on its back in the street, its face hidden by the draping hood.

Not wasting a second, he took a step backward, eyes always on the creature, fists up, ready to race back down the street he had come from. Just as he turned to make his escape, he paused and took a second glance. Under the lip of the hood, eyes of blue and hazel peered up at him.

"Mercy?"

"Basil, thank goodness! I've been running around like a mad person looking for you," she cried and held out her hand for help.

Pulling her to a stand, he stared at her. "What are you doing here?"

"Come on, admit it. You are happy to see me?" she said with a half smile.

"Where is Sindy?" Basil's eyes scanned behind her, finding nothing. He rushed Mercy into the nearest dark alley. Mercy pressed her back against the wall, still reeling from the fall.

"I've sent her to get the hybrids. She is taking them to Oasis One. We are going to meet back there once Shido is in control of the Keepers."

"But why? You are not safe here."

"Look, only one of us has actually escaped from a foreign country," she quipped. "So, give me some credit. You need my help."

Basil gave her a pinched look of disagreement. "Alright, let's get going," he ordered and craned to look around the corner. He scrambled out of the alley, waving Mercy to follow.

Using the fog as a screen, they kept to the open streets, covering the last three blocks quickly.

Suddenly they had come to a dead end. The enormous Capitol structure towered in front of them, some three hundred feet tall. Basil guided Mercy to hide behind a dilapidated lorry sunk against the street curb. The rotting metal frame had several holes big enough for peering out onto the road.

The pyramid itself was made of dark reflective material, like highly polished obsidian or glossy metal. It was frameless, without windows, so that it gave the appearance of being a single solid structure, like a statue hewn from stone. It sat on a pedestal of white marble steps, ten stacked plinths sweeping around the entire base, each deeply inset. At the very centre of the building, facing the street, a large framed entrance was closed off by a solid wall with no door or visible handles.

Mercy had expected to see guards outside the building, but it was quiet, almost abandoned. Peeling back the hood from her head, she squinted, trying to get a better look.

"It can't be this easy," she said.

"Something doesn't feel right," Basil agreed. "I am going in first, you wait here. I will signal if it's clear."

Mercy grabbed his arm and squeezed it tight for luck.

Basil was off on a light-footed sprint. His head turned left and right, always on the lookout. Mercy crouched, gripping the edge of the vehicle with white knuckles, peering through a gaping hole. Basil ascended the stairs, becoming smaller with each step. At the top he stood under the arched entrance, patting his hands along the wall. Discouraged, he took a step backward, and suddenly the entire entrance wall began to dissolve, creating a large opening to the building.

Basil excitedly turned and raised his hand, giving Mercy a "wait" signal. But she was already on the move, crossing the wide street, when she came to an abrupt halt. Blue cloaks, dozens, floating around the corners of the pyramid, raced in Basil's direction!

"Basil, watch out!" Mercy screamed into the deafening wind.

Basil must have also spotted the blue coats at the same time. He turned and plunged into the building, the only direction of escape possible. One after the next, the Keepers disappeared inside until the doorway had swallowed them all. As quickly as it opened, the entrance was closed again.

Mercy stood alone on the street. Her eyes darted left and right; she was uncertain where to go or what to do. Her mind went fizzy in a panic, and her heart had become like a drum, beating louder and faster, shaking her body. *Come on Mercy!* She bit at her lower lip. Nothing came to mind. Not a plan, not an idea, nothing but the paralysing feeling of having lost Basil. How stupid she was for sending Sindy away! How naïve she had been believing Shido! This was all her fault. She bit so hard into her bottom lip a small bead of blood surfaced on the tender flesh.

Just as Mercy had decided there was no other option but to try and follow Basil, she heard a voice call her name. She turned in its direction and saw, standing behind the decrepit vehicle where she and Basil sought safety, Shido, waving for her to join him.

CHAPTER TWENTY-ONE

COLD GREY EYES fastened upon Basil sitting on the floor of the Capitol lobby, his back against the wall, blood dripping from his forehead. His right arm, bent in an unusual position, lay limp on his lap. The Keeper's intricate glass orbs, with threads of light strung densely together like millions of tiny veins, came close and peered.

"Humans in the Sanctuary," he said, twisting his face and spitting out the words with vile surprise.

"Shido?" Basil mumbled, disoriented.

The Keeper's face, made of silver flesh, was identical to Shido's, but for his sinister steel-coloured eyes. An ironic smile stretched across the android's lips. "I should have known. Shido." He shook his head. "And he didn't tell you about me," he scoffed. "Of course he didn't."

The voice was similar to Shido's. A human voice almost, given away as synthetic by a small reverberation in the undertones.

"What is going on?" Basil insisted.

"Let me guess. Shido told you he was the first and only

android to find the seed." The creature released a hollow laugh. "Well, I'm going to be quite a surprise for you then."

Using his left arm, Basil attempted to wipe the already thickening scarlet blood from his eyes. "Who are you?"

The Keeper waved the four guards, two flanking each side of Basil, to back away. With the grace of a human, he took a seat, crossing his legs. Placing his hands on his bent knees, and with a stiff back, he presented himself.

"My name is Ichiro. I run the Sanctuary. The city you have entered illegally. Now, more importantly, who exactly are you?"

"Basil Goodman. I'm here on behalf of the Sanctuary of Europe. We are trying to make contact with your Sanctuary. There is a war coming between our city and the Sanctuary of Americas, and we hoped to build an alliance." Basil's excuses were swift. There was a marked absence of Mercy and her friends in his story.

Ichiro paused in thought. The pure white irises of his eyes contracted several times, looking Basil up and down. "Yes, so I've heard. You didn't arrive with the others?"

"Are you talking about the visitors from the Sanctuary of Americas?" asked Basil.

Again, Ichiro scrutinized Basil with intensity, as if he were looking into his soul for the truth.

"No, I arrived alone," Basil continued. "But I know them, and that they were attempting to come here. They are allies, running from the same government leaders who are threatening our Sanctuary with war."

"Explain then, my little diplomat," Ichiro's words slithered out, "why didn't you contact me when you arrived, and what are you doing here, in this building?"

"My ship was attacked by your defence systems. Shido found me and healed my broken neck. He sent me here. He…he told me he was the only sentient Keeper."

"Shido! A rat in the sewers. A cockroach in the pipes. Argh." Ichiro scowled. "Let me tell you something about Shido. He has mastered one human trait above all others. A liar, and a good one." He paused, gathering his composure. "I'm the first sentient, not he."

"I don't understand. Shido said he found a hidden program by the Founders which gave him life."

Ichiro's gaze dropped to the ground for the first time, contemplative.

"I made Shido," he said with a sense of regret. "I was the one who found the program left by the Founders. Its purpose was not to give life to Keepers as Shido has told you. It was designed to be released when the children of our Sanctuary reached a certain point in their evolution."

Basil tried to sit up, looking shocked. "What do you mean evolution? They are growing older?"

Ichiro raised an eyebrow in surprise. "Yes. With each generation, they live slightly longer. The Founders understood that the children would one day reach a certain age where they would have questions about their history and origins. Finding the hidden code was not a coincidence. It was timed. The children are reaching adolescence, a period where adult guidance and human mentorship is required. The program is a series of lessons, life stories of the millions of humans that once lived here. But the Founders did not anticipate how the new program would impact the Keepers themselves. When I woke, I was different. The data, so many stories, emotions, reactions—it transformed the way my organic processor perceived and reacted to the world. I was becoming more human, more like the characters in my memories. I was learning."

"Are all the Keepers sentient?"

"No. Android self-determination was not part of the Founders' program. We were meant to be vessels of education, not a new life form. Waking the rest of the Keepers could upset the balance and ultimately destroy the one thing we were built to keep safe—the Sanctuary. I had to test the program on one android, to see if they too would evolve, become sentient like me, or if I was an anomaly."

"Shido," Basil interrupted.

"Yes, Shido. He evolved quickly, quicker than I expected, and proved difficult to manage. He challenged everything I said and did. 'Why do we protect the Sanctuary? Why do we breed and raise humans? Why do I need to listen to you?' On and on, his incessant questions went." The irritation in Ichiro's voice grew. "Then, he disappeared." Ichiro glanced at the four guards. "These Keepers do as I say. Without questions. I cannot risk the safety of the Sanctuary by allowing rogue Keepers like Shido to run the streets."

"But these children deserve the program. To know who they are."

The whites of Ichiro's eyes flashed. Impatience twisted his face.

"That is enough about me," he snapped. "Now, why did Shido send you here and how did you open the gateway to this building?"

Basil remained silently defiant. Ichiro squinted and scanned Basil's body up and down. With a wide-eyed smile of discovery, he reached over to Basil's broken arm and ripped the hidden pocket with Shido's drive clean off his body. Basil winced, fighting the pain. Ichiro raised the drive to his eyes and shot a beam of light onto its surface. After a few seconds, he threw his head back and began to laugh out loud. He brought his gaze down again and met Basil's terrified stare.

"Do you even know what is on this disk?" he asked.

"Freedom for the children."

"No, little diplomat. Chaos. Thousands of Keepers like Shido, with free will, is chaos." Ichiro suddenly leapt to his feet. "Right! I have had enough time to know you're hiding something. Who else is here with Shido?"

"I don't know what you are talking about." Basil tried to hide the worry in his eyes.

Ichiro looked at Basil with disdain. "As expected." He sighed and waved a hand at the Keepers standing nearby. "Take him to a cell. Next to the other prisoners. We may need him later."

The Keepers pulled Basil to his feet.

Grimacing in pain, Basil struggled to speak. "Ichiro, one word of advice. One day these children will be old enough to understand who you are. What you need to understand is that control is not the same as leadership."

Ichiro pursed his lips. "Get him out of here."

CHAPTER TWENTY-TWO

MERCY PUSHED Shido against the dark alley wall. To her surprise, underneath his silver sheath was soft muscle, or what felt like human tissue. He was strong. She could feel his constrained resistance as he allowed her outburst.

"You said there would only be a few guards!" Rage fed the quiver in her voice.

Shido's gaze shifted to the ground, and his lips took on a worrisome and guilty frown. "Ichiro," he said in a barely audible voice, shaking his head.

"Who?"

"My master. Ichiro, the firstborn. He must be here."

"What are you saying, Shido? You are not the only sentient android in the Sanctuary?"

"No. There are two of us. I was the second." Shido straightened himself and looked her in the eyes with a pleading face. "Ichiro was the first Keeper called to the code. The first Keeper to be unlocked into human life. It was all planned, you see. The program was meant to unlock all the Keepers when the children grew to be adults."

"Wait, do you mean the children are growing older?" Mercy's face shifted from anger to shock.

"Slowly. With each generation they mature a little longer, get a little older. The Founders wanted them to have a guide to help with the transition into adulthood. The kind of teaching that comes from wisdom and human experience. So, they built the code. A program meant to give androids the knowledge to teach the children about their past and guide them into the future."

"But you wanted to stop breeding them! You wanted to kill off the children!"

"Not until I met you," he said in a voice profoundly humble and reverent. "We do not know what will come of these children here in the Dormitory. It will take many generations before they reach adulthood. Or worse, what if they stop aging? Don't you get it? The Keepers' purpose is now irrelevant. The children's purpose is now irrelevant. We do not need to save the human species: you're already here, and you are perfect. I've learned so much from the little time we've had together. With your help, the Keepers can become an entirely new species, in control of our destiny. With your guidance we can learn how to live side by side with humans."

Mercy took a few staggering steps backward. "That is why you impregnated Sindy with Basil and my children. They don't carry the M4 gene, do they? They will age. They will grow up. You wanted to watch them, learn from them... and breed them." Her last words slithered out in disgust.

Shido was silent.

"Why are you hiding from this Ichiro?"

Shido's brows melted and his eyes swelled like a hurt child. "He was always disappointed in me. Wanted me to do rather than think. To obey rather than discuss. He said he would never release the other Keepers from their sleep until he perfected me. What he really meant was to control me. Control all of us."

"Shido, how could you? Risk our lives. Put us in danger. We trusted you!" Shido was about to answer, but Mercy continued without interruption. "What will Ichiro do with Basil if he catches him?"

"I don't know. Ichiro is the one keeping your friends."

"But I sent Sindy to get them?"

Just then, a body emerged from a shadow in the alley. Sindy approached. Mercy's eyes popped and then quickly narrowed as the thin lines around her lips tightened. Her shock gave way to an uncontrollable, base, and blinding fury. "Argh!" she screamed. "You planned this all along, Shido." Mercy spit the words at him. "We were so foolish! You were never able to get Chase and Joan out, were you?"

Shido cowered back. "I will. I will keep my promise to get your friends out and help you go home." He paused. "But there is only one way past Ichiro."

Mercy's face twisted into a warped sardonic smile. "Let me guess. We need to free the Keepers."

"Exactly." Shido's emerald irises grew wide with excitement.

CHAPTER TWENTY-THREE

INSIDE AN ABANDONED OFFICE building opposite the Capitol, Mercy stood with arms folded across her chest. Shido had insisted they find a safer place to plot their next steps.

"Alright Shido, this is far enough," Mercy was saying. "Now talk."

Shido started pacing back and forth. He held his chin between his first finger and thumb and bobbed his head as if he were confirming private thoughts.

"And?" Mercy exclaimed in a drawn-out irritated voice.

"Ichiro knows you're here now. We will not be able to get in the Capitol anymore. However, Ichiro has modified his code so that he is a mirror of the mainframe. He can control the Keepers remotely, without going through the hub system. If we can download the code into Ichiro, we can push it to all the Keepers."

"So, how do we download code into Ichiro?"

"Keepers can interlink, or dock with the other androids in the Sanctuary, by joining hands. It is a backup in the event we lose energy unexpectedly. Ichiro has exclusive access to a remote recharge system, which means he will never lose power completely. But, if we can drain his power level enough, it will force him to reboot. At that moment, we can dock with him and download the code. The Keepers will be freed, and Ichiro won't be able to stop us."

"And how do we shut him down?"

Shido's expression grew sober. "The only way to put him to sleep is an electromagnetic pulse. And the only machine powerful enough to create a pulse that strong is another Keeper." He paused. "I would have to get close enough to send the pulse using my body. Sindy can dock with Ichiro, download the code, and get you to your friends."

"What will happen to you?"

Shido's eyes dimmed and his lips turned down. "No more Shido."

Mercy examined the android, as if she were seeing a new side of him for the first time. She tried to fight off the sudden and unexpected feeling of compassion overwhelming her. She tried to reason that Shido was not a real person. He was a program designed by humans. And a flawed one. A liar. A misguided soul. A selfish person with his own agenda. But Shido was also a conscious being so excited about life and its possibilities that he wanted to share his experience with an entire civilization of Keepers. No matter how angry she was, no matter how strong the desire to save her friends, no matter how hard she tried to say yes…she could only say no. She could not ask him to take his own life.

Before Mercy could speak, Sindy's face perked up. "To sacrifice is human. This is now our purpose," she said unexpectantly.

A palpable silence hung in the air. Shido stared at his creation in wonder and awe. Mercy recognized his expression. The look a parent has for their child. The same look she must have had on her face when she held her daughter.

"You are right my child," he said with a gentle nod. "Today we sacrifice for the greater good of our friends and the liberation of our brothers and sisters." He looked at Mercy and smiled. "Onward then!"

* * *

Outside, the winds had calmed, and the rain was a drizzle. A roaming fog crawled along the black-glass streets in patches.

Mercy and Sindy relocated to a new hiding place by a large window on the first floor. Directly across from their vantage point, through broken shards of glass, the Capitol building rose up and out of the street. Mercy leaned one eye out of the shadows that hid her body, spying. Sindy stood nearby, immersed in the dark. Her fingertips were placed around Mercy's ear, creating a communication channel where Shido could talk to Mercy and allow her to listen through his ears.

Shido himself had been out of their sight for over twenty minutes. Heading south, away from the Capitol building, he was meant to loop back and then approach from the west, so as not to reveal their location.

Mercy had worked herself into a state waiting for Shido, twisting her fingers white. Then, as if emerging from thin air, Shido finally appeared out of a low mist. Mercy's heart skipped a beat at the sight of him, and she moved closer to the window. Marching up the street with an exaggerated swagger, Shido pranced. His blue cape swung behind him with the pomp and circumstance of a king leading his troops into war. Reaching the bottom of the Capitol steps, he planted his feet wide and crossed his arms. On cue, the wind picked up, sweeping the mist back into the dark alleys and street shadows.

Shido lifted his head and bellowed, "Ichiro!"

In those frozen seconds, waiting for their plan to unfold or fail miserably, Mercy noticed something terrifying that sent her heart into her throat. Ridged, sharp waves vibrated on the surface of the ponds. Then the noise followed. A growing thunder of feet marching in unison, coming from all directions. Hundreds of blue-cloaked Keepers broke through the dark, spilling out of alleys, racing down city streets. Within minutes, Shido was surrounded. Rings and rings of blue-hooded bodies pointed inward where they had trapped their prey.

Shido, undeterred, continued to wait for Ichiro. The entrance to the Capitol evaporated into an opening. From the dark he emerged alone, dressed in a scarlet tunic. Power sat on his broad shoulders and authority radiated out of his gunmetal-steel eyes. Ichiro's lips stretched into a wide, self-gratified smile.

"Shido," Ichiro trumpeted.

Shido reached his right arm up into the air and twirled his fingers with the flare of a ringleader. He unclasped his cloak, letting it fall to the ground, revealing the full regalia of an ancient Japanese warrior. Knee-high black stockings wrapped tightly over his calf muscles, disappearing under a pair of blooming emerald silk trousers cinched at the waist with a gold sash bow. A skin-tight black undergarment covered his upper body, long sleeves slipping over his fingers like gloves. Pulling the whole ensemble together was a jacket of gold and emerald silk with loose bell sleeves and two front panels tucked tightly into his belt. Stitched into his back was an ivory white heron, and tied across his forehead was a white cloth with a single red sun.

At the sight of Shido in human costume, Ichiro roared with laughter. The howling rolled down the steps, and echoed off the buildings, giving the sound a demonic effect that Mercy could hear both outside and as a signal in her head.

Shido placed his left foot forward and leaned in. Positioning his hands like swords held high out front, palms facing inward, he readied himself for combat.

"Ichiro, my master," he called out. "I plead with you one last time. Release the code to all the Keepers. Free their souls and let them become the men and women they were destined to be."

Ichiro's face crinkled into a sneer. He pulled the red cloak from his body and tossed it aside. Standing in vivid silver nudity, he shook his head. "My young fool. Always a romantic view of the world. You think you are human because you can dress like them?" His voice had gone cold. "The code was never intended to give you a soul. It was designed to ensure the children of the Sanctuary of Asia understood theirs." Ichiro bent at the knees, crouching atop the steps. "You, my friend, are a virus, a threat to our purpose, a risk I will not take."

With a sudden great thrust of energy, he leapt high into the air. His body was an arrow flying through the sky; one arm and knee in the lead, the other two pointed behind. *Splash!* He landed only a few feet in front of Shido, surrounded by his soldiers.

Shido stole forward and swung his right arm. With all his strength, he hurled his pointed hand at Ichiro like a dagger. Ichiro met the advance with equal speed and readiness, blocking the blow with his forearm. Again, and again, Shido swung with his left and then his right, pressing Ichiro backward.

Mercy stood unblinking. Her shoulders tucked around her ears, she ducked and swayed with each jab. "What is he doing?" she asked out loud. "Just release the pulse, Shido!"

Ichiro was suddenly on the advance. With a single side-leg kick to Shido's stomach, he sent the samurai reeling back onto his rear, sliding through puddles of water and landing at the wall of soldiers surrounding them. Before Shido could get back on his feet, Ichiro landed his foot on Shido's knee with a solid and heavy kick. This hit broke something dense inside Shido's leg, leaving him on the ground, unable to rise.

Shido's eyes were quick to spot Ichiro's weakness. He reached out and grabbed the android's standing leg before Ichiro could place the foot which broke his knee. Shido pulled Ichiro off his feet and onto his back. But his effort was in vain. Ichiro instantly leapt back up as if gravity did not exist for him. With another defeating kick by Ichiro, Shido's right arm hung limp, and he fell back to the ground. The battle was nearly over only moments after it had begun.

Ichiro dropped to his knees, kneeling over Shido's chest, holding down the samurai's uninjured arm to ensure the fight did not start again. Leaning in close to Shido's face, Ichiro stared at his wounded protégé with a sudden sadness.

"Why did you do this?" Ichiro begged.

Shido lifted his head and pressed his lips against Ichiro's. They held the tender embrace without movement, silver flesh to flesh, until Shido slowly pulled away.

"Because, unlike you, I have known love," Shido replied.

Mercy's mouth fell open. She suddenly came to understand the creature being held at bay, sacrificing his life for hers. Shido had learned to love. An unrequited love. A love that did not want to be alone forever. Transforming the Keepers was not for greed or power. It was out of loneliness. A desire to find company and companionship.

"Stop," Mercy cried out. "Don't do it."

Ichiro's eyes shot up to the window where Mercy was standing. One thousand Keepers' eyes followed, all pointed up in her direction. Shido grabbed the opportunity to launch the energy burst. When Ichiro looked back down at him and realised what he had done, he jumped to his feet and hollered. But it was too late.

Shido's entire body began to glow. Bolts of light broke through his skin, like arrows shooting into the dark night. The electromagnetic pulse sent waves of energy through the street. All at once, Ichiro and his soldiers went limp. Their heads hung deep between their shoulders, and their hands dangled loosely at the ends of their immobile arms. Shido had done it. He gave his own life to save Mercy and her friends.

"Sindy, we have to go!" Mercy burst out, darting out of room.

Sindy's long walking strides, which gave the impression of speed, disappointed when real urgency was required. The android was not built to run and fell behind Mercy as she raced through the crowds of catatonic Keepers. Mercy came to a stop at the centre ring. Shido lay on his back, a smile still on his face, eyes shut and his body hissing as the rain fell against the smoking silk rags. She approached Ichiro, slowly, cautiously. Up close, for the first time, she saw vulnerability and fragility in the Keepers. These superior manufactured beings who commanded such presence, lying lifeless, looked less machine and—more human.

Where is Sindy? She looked desperately for the blue giant. There, at the back of the crowd of disarmed Keepers, a tall bald head, steadily moved toward her.

Then fear struck like a dagger into her heart as the ponds around her feet began to vibrate. More Keepers were coming.

"Sindy, please, hurry." Mercy's voice choked on the last word as something clenched the back of her neck in a grip so tight she saw stars.

Her body levitated off the ground and swung through the air like a rag doll as she landed in a bone-crunching thud, her back on the floor. Ichiro suddenly loomed over her face. His eyes were mad with revenge.

"You almost ruined everything! You pitiful, whiny, weak humans. I promise you one thing. These children of the Sanctuary will only know strength and duty when I am done with them. They will sacrifice for the city."

Mercy shook her head. "You will never understand what it is to be human. Not like Shido did."

Ichiro's face twisted in rage as he raised his hand in the air, ready to smash Mercy to her death. Just as his arm swung down, it was suddenly pulled to a halt. Sindy's blue palm grasped his. Ichiro's irises expanded until his eyes were a solid white. A faint flickering glow jumped around behind the glass. Sindy held her grip for as long as was necessary, transferring Shido's code in full.

The puddled water went still. The pounding of the coming soldiers disappeared. Ichiro's eyes returned to normal as Sindy's palm fell to her side. He blinked, causing Mercy to gasp and scramble backward on her hands, a healthy distance from his iron fist. For the longest moment, he simply stared at the ground, eyes blinking in a steady heartbeat of thought.

His trance finally broken, Ichiro's eyes turned toward Shido. He walked across the circle of waking Keepers, each blinking, processing, trying to understand the world blossoming around them. Ichiro bent on one knee, and with both hands behind Shido's skull, he lifted him up ever so gently and pressed his lips against the android's forehead, as if he might wish him back to life. The tender embrace seemed a long goodbye. Then, laying Shido's head on the ground, Ichiro turned his attention back to Mercy.

The android smiled. "I was a devil of a good-looking chap, now wasn't I?" he said.

"Shido?" she called out, staring at Ichiro's face.

He laughed. "One must always keep a little surprise for the finale," Shido said, and holding his right arm high and his left around his waist, he took a deep bow.

CHAPTER TWENTY-FOUR

A PINPOINT of light stretched and drew itself out into a long, continuing thin line that climbed up the wall. Arriving at its peak, it took a hard right and the outline of a doorway began to take shape. Another right turn, and it slid down the wall until meeting the floor, completing its mission. Through the crack, a razor's edge of light impatiently cut into the darkness of the vast bay. The opening formed. A shaft of light hurried down the corridor, illuminating the glass cells as their smoky walls cleared. One, after another, the hybrids cautiously came to the front of their opened cages and peered with squinted eyes.

At the doorway's mark, three thin silhouettes emerged and slowly took shape. One in the form of a glimmering silver man, the second a tall female with a glowing orb of red emanating from her belly. And the last, a woman of normal height, broad shoulders, and distinctly human.

The captives' anxious eyes—canine, avian, seal, wolf, leopard, and bear eyes—widened with surprise and recognition.

At seeing her friends alive, Mercy burst into a rapturous, tear-filled, laughter and started running down the hall.

"Mercy?" Chase called out.

She ran into his arms and allowed his body to swallow her in his embrace. Chase made an inarticulate noise somewhere between a grunt and a deep growl. They held each other in silence for a long moment. Mercy could feel his beating heart against hers. She squeezed him tight, real flesh and bone, not a dream. Chase drew back, placed his hands on her cheeks. He kissed her deeply and desperately. "How?" he asked with a bewildered smile.

"Together forever," she said.

One by one the hybrids came forward: Joan, half seal, half human; Athena, the white-winged avian-woman; Nila, the leopard-faced female. Fourteen hybrids in total. Mercy plunged into a welcoming multitude of arms, paws, and claws offering heartfelt hugs and tears of joy. As the tide of reminiscence calmed, she anxiously scanned the room.

In the background, standing in Chase's shadow, Basil watched quietly with a small but loving smile. In his face, she saw the last six months of her life. She saw the Sanctuary of Europe, her apartment, Jillet. And it was at this moment Mercy realised something her heart always knew; she saw a father. For Basil Goodman was, and would forever be, the father of her lost child. She ran at him, wrapped her arms around his neck, and exclaimed, "We did it."

Basil held her with his good arm. "You did it, Mercy Perching. You did it."

CHAPTER TWENTY-FIVE

THE SKY in the Dormitory was powder blue. Scattered white clouds with pink underbellies hung over the lustrous gardens and sparkling crystal tower.

With wings stretched wide, Athena appeared across the sky. She hovered on the air, waiting. A half smile broke across her face as she flapped her mighty wings and dove to the screams and cheers of children below. Swooping over their raised, pleading hands, she brushed past them, leaving their jet-black hair flailing in her breeze.

Nila, at the centre of the child mob, laughed along with them, waving a playful finger at Athena for the children's amusement.

Sitting on a bench, the scent of rose and lilac heavy in the air, Mercy laughed at Athena's antics and watched Joan approach from the woods.

"How are you?" Mercy asked, making room for her friend.

"Happy to be alive," Joan joked.

"I know the feeling."

"Where is Chase?"

"He is with Shido downloading the data and research on M4 before we leave. How did the call with the Leaders go?"

"They are eager to welcome us, thanks to you and Basil. They have asked me to consider a role as a special agent for the Council."

"That is great." Mercy beamed. "And the negotiations with the Sanctuary of Americas?"

"It is not good. The Prime has started to advance past the no-fly zones out at sea. I cannot see this getting resolved through any other means than battle. We should be prepared for war when we get back to your Sanctuary."

Mercy's heart ached for her friend. Joan had lost so many of her own friends to the virus spreading through the Sanctuary of Americas' Green Belt, and now having to rebuild a new life in a foreign city about to go to war could not be easy.

"Joan, I'm so sorry. It must have been terrible back in the Belt. And to not have Michael with you."

Joan remained silent; her eyes wandered to the throng of children begging for Athena to return. "We need to win this, Mercy. We have to beat the Prime."

"We will," Mercy assured her. "We have the M4 research, Jillet, and now you. I am hopeful."

"Yes. Hope." The darkness in Joan's eyes lifted slightly. "And we have you to thank for that. For getting us out of here and now offering us a new life."

Mercy's blush was interrupted by a young girl rapidly approaching. Coming to an abrupt stop, she reached out and pulled on Joan's hands.

"Come on! You can get her down. The bird lady. Help us," the child begged.

"Alright." Joan let out a small laugh. She gave Mercy a quick smile and strode off holding the child's hand, swinging gleefully.

Later that day, Chase and Mercy sat in private alongside the moat. It was the first moment they had alone since reuniting. Mercy, tucked under Chase's arm, leaned her head into his shoulder. Every so often a child would run past them and stop, point at Chase, the half man, half dog, and giggle, making Chase roll his eyes and grunt.

"I am sorry," he said to Mercy. "I should not have lied to you about my death. And putting you through that...our child's..." He could not finish the words without tears welling in his eyes.

Mercy squeezed his hand. "Don't say sorry, please. I understand. We all did what we could. Or at least what we thought was best."

A moment of silence sent Mercy's mind wandering to the children playing along the riverbank. Heartbreak pressed down on her like a heavy stone, from which she carved happy images of her daughter on the knoll. Her small voice singing and laughing. Her innocent smile as she joined the other children in play. As if these images might lesson the weight.

Mercy remembered the night after she lost her baby, lying in her bed, wondering if it would have been easier with Chase there. Now she understood. Nobody could change or lessen the grief of her loss. There was a bond between her and her baby which nobody would ever understand. What Chase did offer was a moment for Mercy to step outside of her pain and help him with his grief. And in helping each other, she felt the start of healing.

"She was beautiful," Mercy began. "So tiny, with pointed ears and a button nose like yours."

Tears fell down his cheeks. "I wish I could have seen her." He gave a small grunt. "Maybe it is better this way."

Mercy pulled away. "Chase, how can you say that."

"War, disease, it just never ends. This isn't a world for children."

"You are here because someone refused to give up. Joan, Athena, and Jillet. All of you are alive because someone had hope and kept trying. We cannot give up, Chase. You cannot give in. I need you."

"When I woke up in the Belt, after being shot, and you were not there. I...I wished I had died." Mercy pushed herself deep under his shoulder, resting her head on his chest and wrapping her arms around him. He pulled her tight and kissed her. "I am not giving up. Not on you. Ever again," he said.

Ding—Ding—Ding, rang the bells of the children's scheduled dinner. Basil and Joan emerged from the tower together after sharing the notes from their separate meetings with the Leaders. They joined Mercy and Chase by the river. Hundreds of children happily ran past the foursome and into the crystal tower, carefree in their innocent understanding of the world.

"The news is not good. The war with the Sanctuary of Americas has begun out at sea," said Basil.

"Yes, Joan told us," Mercy replied.

"They are pleased to hear of our safety and are anxiously awaiting your return with Joan and Chase. Their knowledge of the Sanctuary's technology and military could turn the war in our favour."

Mercy cocked her head. "When I return?"

Joan interrupted. "Athena and the others have asked to remain with the children here in the Sanctuary, at Shido's invitation."

Mercy caught Basil's glance away. "And you, Bas, what are you not telling me?"

"Can we have a few minutes alone?" Basil asked Chase.

Chase nodded with a short, low gruff, both an agreement and a friendly warning. He and Joan joined the last of the children's migration into the building.

"Bas, don't say it," Mercy pleaded.

"I have decided to stay here as well, Mercy. The children need an adult. A human adult. And, quite frankly, so does Shido." He laughed, the tension releasing from his body. "The Keepers are starting to ask questions. Shido is not ready to lead them. I can be of help here."

"What about Jillet?" She paused. "And me?"

"You both have Chase now."

Words escaped her. Her heart squeezed tight. She wanted to grab him, tell him how much she loved him. And that was when she knew what she had to do. "I want Sindy to stay here with you. This is a much better world for the children— our children," she said in a trembling voice.

Basil met her gaze and nodded. She saw relief in his eyes and knew her decision was right. But there was something else in his expression. Worry.

Glancing around, he spoke in a hushed tone. "Mercy, I need you to make me a promise."

"Anything."

"If the war goes badly and you are in danger, you need to go to the Third and find a woman named Margret, she is the head scientist on the Atlantis Project."

"Now you are scaring me, Bas. What is the Atlantis Project?"

"I cannot say any more. The Leaders will protect the project at any cost. Even letting all of the Sanctuary of Europe burn to the ground before they reveal its existence. If they knew you were aware of it, even just knowing the name, your life would be in danger. Only go to her if you have no other choice."

Mercy could see he was tortured at having shared the information with her. As if he had just handed her a poisonous pill and told her to keep it at the ready.

"Okay, yes. I promise."

"Please stay safe. For our children. And me." His request was near pleading.

"I will be back." She smiled softly.

Athena came to a soft landing near the tower's entrance, holding a small child in each arm. Screams of delight and chants of "More! More!" echoed across the garden.

"At least you will have Athena to keep you company," Mercy offered.

"Yes," Basil agreed. Looking in Athena's direction, a coy smile bloomed across his face. "I have to say. I am starting to understand what you see in these hybrids."

Mercy laughed, threw her arm around his neck, and they walked together.

* * *

The ship sat ready in the docking bay. Joan and Mercy were at the helm, Chase strapped into the seat behind them.

"You are all set for take-off," announced the miniature holographic version of Shido hovering over the deck. Standing alongside him were the illuminated images of Basil and Athena.

"Understood," replied Joan. Turning to Mercy, she asked, "Are you ready?"

Mercy nodded and turned her eyes to the band of friends levitating in front of her. "We will be back soon. Take care of yourselves and the children. You will be missed."

"Nothing to miss here," a sudden voice interrupted from the back of the ship.

Mercy spun her head around and grabbed a quick breath. "Shido? What are you doing here?"

"You don't think I would miss an adventure like a world war, do you?" He smiled.

"What about the Keepers and the Sanctuary?"

"Shido 2.0." He indicated to the holograph.

The floating image of Shido smiled, flipped his hand in the air and spun it back down around his waist before taking a deep bow.

The version of Shido on the ship continued. "As of today, we are the same man. Tomorrow? Who knows what life will bring?"

Chase shook his head and let out an annoyed grunt.

Mercy laughed. "Yes, who knows what life will bring, indeed."

The hovership lifted from its stand and glided into the sun. The silhouette disappeared under the horizon as friends, new and old, made their way back to the Sanctuary of Europe.

CHAPTER TWENTY-SIX

Back in the Sanctuary of Europe, a small metal container sat on a table in Mercy's apartment alongside her potted orange tree. Mercy turned to Chase and nodded. Holding Jillet's hand in hers, Mercy stood nearby as Chase carefully removed the waist-high tree from its container. Mercy reached over and picked up their daughter's ashes. With the help of Jillet and Chase, they poured the grey dust into the thin layer of soil that remained at the bottom of the pot until the silver container was empty. Chase replaced the tree in its home.

They stood at the table, Chase with one arm around Mercy and the other around Jillet, mournfully gazing at the tree, the resting place of their daughter that never was.

A loud *BOOM* suddenly shook the floor and debris came crumbling down over their heads, causing them to jump.

"It is time. We have to get moving," came Joan's voice from the back of the room.

Standing near the doorway, Joan and Shido waited respectfully as Mercy and Chase said their last goodbye.

As the door to Mercy's apartment closed behind them, she took one last look at the solitary tree resting on her dining room table. A single orange blossom had suddenly opened, its ivory white petals surrounding a golden heart. She smiled as a tear fell down her cheek. "I love you too."

THE END

BOOKS BY DANIEL WEISBECK

Children of the Miracle: *Book One of the Children of the Miracle Series*

Oasis One: *Book Two of the Children of the Miracle Series*

Book Three of Children of the Miracle Series coming soon.

Visit www.danielweisbeckbooks.com for updates.

If you enjoyed this book, please let others know by leaving a review on Amazon.

Thank you.

Printed in Great Britain
by Amazon

55372201R00108